SECOND CHANCE AT LOVE™

DIANA MORGAN

BLONDES PREFER GENTLEMEN

AF538428

BERKLEY BOOKS, NEW YORK

BLONDES PREFER GENTLEMEN

Copyright © 1988 by Irene Goodman and Alex Kamaroff

All rights reserved. No part of this publication may be reproduced or transmitted in any form or by any means, electronic or mechanical, including photocopy, recording, or any information storage and retrieval system, without permission in writing from the publisher.

Requests for permission to make copies of any part of the work should be mailed to: Permissions, Second Chance at Love, The Berkley Publishing Group, 200 Madison Avenue, New York, NY 10016.

First edition published December 1988

ISBN: 0-425-11199-7

"Second Chance at Love" and the butterfly emblem are trademarks belonging to Jove Publications, Inc. The name "BERKLEY" and the "B" logo are trademarks belonging to Berkley Publishing Corporation.

Second Chance at Love books are published by
The Berkley Publishing Group
200 Madison Avenue, New York, NY 10016

Printed in the United States of America

10 9 8 7 6 5 4 3 2 1

"Ah, alone at last," James said to himself, reaching for the glass of champagne.

A subtle noise behind him caused him to look up. James heard a distinct footstep, sat up sharply—and froze.

A pixie was standing at the front of the room. The vision was scanning over the tables one at a time as if looking for something she had lost. She could not have been more than five feet in height, with a delicate little face, a cloud of golden hair that just touched her shoulders, and a belted gray wool cape that hid most of her tiny form.

She still hadn't noticed James in the dim light of the immense room. From under her jacket, she removed a large sack, which she shook open; and then she proceeded over to the waiter's station, where two steaks were waiting to be served. To James's utter amazement, the pixie removed a large plastic container from her sack and lifted the steaks with the pair of tongs beside them. She was just about to place the meat inside the container when the sound of James's voice made her freeze.

"I believe those were just about to be served to the Winchesters."

Startled, she whipped around, giving him a look of wild alarm.

"If you really need to eat," he continued cordially, "then perhaps you'll join me . . ."

Diana Morgan

Diana Morgan is a pseudonym for a husband-and-wife team who only moonlight as writers. By day they are two of New York's busiest literary agents. They met at a phone booth at Columbia University in 1977, and have been together romantically and professionally ever since.

"We began writing together strictly by accident," they confess, "deriving our pen name from our cat, Dinah Cat Morgenstern." Writing turned out to be a welcome form of comic relief from the pressures of business.

"This is a wonderful opportunity for us to talk directly to you, the reader. Our books have often been described as humorous or zany, but we feel there is an underlying seriousness to even our craziest story. What we hope to convey is a certain joie de vivre that will escape from the pages into a part of your life."

The "Morgans" enjoy all kinds of music, pigging out, small children and elves (especially their children, Robbie and Elizabeth), and trying to figure out what will happen next on Dallas.

Other Second Chance at Love books by
Diana Morgan

ANYTHING GOES #286
TWO IN A HUDDLE #309
BRINGING UP BABY #329
POCKETFUL OF MIRACLES #354
TO CATCH A THIEF #377
THE WEDDING BELLE #403
STRANGER THAN FICTION #444

Dear Reader:

Come in from the cold and warm yourself with this month's romances from Second Chance at Love. In *All the Flowers* (#452) author Mary Modean pens a beautiful story of a love come home. And Second Chance at Love veteran author Diana Morgan takes us on board a luxury liner for all kinds of intrigue in *Blondes Prefer Gentlemen* (#453).

There's no such thing as an ex-love. Joanna McKenna assuages any doubt of that when she pays a surprise visit to the law office of her ex-husband, Jerrod. Unsure of what she expects from him, or herself, Joanna *is* sure of only one thing—she loves Jerrod, she always has and always will. Though Jerrod's thrilled that Joanna's back, he's scared to death. After all, most of the problems they once had haven't ever gone away. His law practice is busier than ever and his daughter not only demands his spare time, but insists on isolating Joanna from their lives. As much as she wants to fit into Jerrod's new life, will she be able to convince him—and herself—that she won't let their troubles chase her away again? *All the Flowers* (#452) will have you believing in "happily ever after."

When a beautiful stowaway meets a handsome cruise ship passenger in *Blondes Prefer Gentlemen* (#453), it's anything but smooth sailing! Free-spirited Susan Melinka is a beautiful blonde with a sense of adventure, a penchant for fun, and an absolutely empty pocket. James William Bentley is a wealthy, down-to-earth, very bored passenger on the liner Susan has secretly picked to take her home. As soon as James discovers Susan making a grab for his dinner, his doldrums are over, only to be replaced by scandal. It seems that more than just steak and champagne are being lifted from the passengers on board. Surely Susan isn't the culprit? Turbulent waters, stormy passion and charming surprises await all in this delightful romp.

Also from The Berkley Publishing Group this fine December is *Nightwylde* by Kimberleigh Caitlin. From the author of *Sky of Ashes, Sea of Flames* comes a passion as hauntingly beautiful as an Irish ballad. A country torn by the flames of rebellion, Ireland held the destiny of Maryssa Wylder—a woman scorned for her willful spirit, and banished from the social whirl of London. Tade Kilcannon, a gentle, kind and handsome man, touched Maryssa's heart with his glorious dreams of freedom—and his penetrating gaze . . . But, a rival, a masked patriot known only as the Black Falcon aroused a burning passion in Maryssa. Soon, her life, her heart and soul, were trapped in a web of intrigue, and torn by her wildest longings. And the author of *Ondine*, Shannon Drake, now brings you *Lie Down in Roses*, a passionate tale of love and intrigue. Torn by the raging fury of the War of the Roses and the searing desires of their own hearts, Lady Genevieve and Lord Tristan—their destiny challenged by deception, revenge, and intrigue—dared to embrace the most treacherous love of all. For fans of Judith Krantz, *Winners and Lovers* by Hilary S. Kayle delves into the love and lust, power and money of the New York publishing world. It's a fast-paced world of high-powered, high-pressured wheeling and dealing. Here, the right connections can lead straight to success; the right parties and talk shows can make or break careers. Only three weeks on the road can turn business into unexpected pleasure . . . The place: Manhattan. The goal: having it all. Finally, acclaimed author Judith Kelman brings us another heart-stopping suspense story, *While Angels Sleep.* "A fascinating thriller . . . and a genuinely surprising finish," says author Barbara Michaels about this novel from the author of *Where Shadows Fall.* Strange, terrible things had happened at Emily's childhood home of Thornwood. There was her mother's sudden death. And her father's slow descent into madness. The pain had ended . . . or so Emily had thought. Now, years later, she has returned—with children of her own. Back to the dark, wooded seclusion of the old artists' colony—where the sins of the past still linger in the shadows, threatening to shatter her cherished family, and her life.

That does it for now! Plenty of great books to keep you sated until next month. Until then, keep warm and . . .

Happy Reading!

Sincerely,

Hillary Cige, Editor
SECOND CHANCE AT LOVE
The Berkley Publishing Group
200 Madison Avenue
New York, NY 10016

To Saralee and Robin,
two free spirits

CHAPTER *One*

UNDER A FULL APRIL moon, the sighting of an iceberg is a thrilling event for one who is traveling across the Atlantic Ocean on a luxury liner. But for James William Bentley, enjoying a leisurely late-night dinner in the first-class dining room, the purser's cry of a triple sighting was nothing more than a signal for all the other diners to rush outside, leaving him alone to ponder an otherwise uneventful vacation. He had seen icebergs before. He had seen everything.

The voices of his uncle Henry, who was traveling with him from London to New York, and his friend Zeebo Molinari, an art collector, wafted in from the deck, where they had gone with everyone else to look at the iceberg.

"I'm just worried about my paintings," Zeebo was saying in his nasal, plaintive tone. "I've got some priceless works of art aboard this ship. If what the captain says is true, I'm hiring an extra security guard."

"Now, now," Henry said, his cut-glass British voice pleasantly moderated. "It's probably just a series of unrelated petty thefts. No need to be unduly alarmed."

James was only half listening to this piece of news. If there really was a thief on board, he felt he probably should lock up his valuables, but he couldn't bring himself to care. Besides, James didn't possess any valuables that couldn't be immediately replaced. Still, his mind wandered idly over the people he had met, wondering if any of them could be guilty of such a crime. It was possible, he supposed. You just never knew sometimes.

He put down his glass of champagne, checked to be doubly sure that no one was around to watch, undid his silk bow tie, and unfastened the top stud of his dress shirt. Now thoroughly pleased with himself, he propped his feet up on the chair opposite him, and leaned back to enjoy the solitude.

"Ah, alone at last," he said to himself, reaching for the glass of champagne. "To solitude," he toasted. "To solitude, and to loneliness, my two favorite drinking companions."

As he sat there sipping the vintage with an ironic grin on his face, a cold breeze suddenly wafted in, rushing across his back. He turned and noticed that one of the portholes was open, the curtains blowing like unfurled flags in the draft.

"I could have sworn that was closed a minute ago," he thought.

It was odd; but he wasn't about to get up to close it. Someone else could close the window later. He was just too comfortable. He turned back and settled into a relaxed position, trying not to think about the pressing business that awaited him in New York. Once he had found it stimulating. He couldn't recall when it had turned into a relentless grind.

A subtle noise behind him caused him to look up. Probably something shifting from the motion of the ship. But then he heard a distinct footstep, sat up sharply—and froze.

He had company.

A pixie was standing at the front of the room.

James blinked a few times, certain the apparition would disappear, but there she remained, standing perfectly still. The vision was scanning the tables one at a time as if looking for something she had lost. She could not have been more than five feet in height, with a delicate little face, a cloud of golden hair that just touched her shoulders, a belted gray wool cape that hid most of her tiny form, and a pair of black Chinese slippers with straps across the insteps. Had he not been paying attention, he might have mistaken her for a child. But this was no child.

He studied her more closely, noticing that she endearingly had put her index finger between her teeth and was biting hard as she seemed to be contemplating her next move. Very carefully, she began to untie her belt, her eyes watching furtively for any movement.

She still hadn't noticed him in the dim light of the immense room, and James sat perfectly still, not making a sound.

From under her jacket, she removed a large sack, which she shook open; and then she proceeded over to the waiter's station, where two steaks were waiting to be served.

James saw her eyes light up, and then his own widened in astonishment. To his utter amazement, the pixie removed a large plastic container from inside the sack and lifted the steaks with the pair of tongs beside them. She was just about to place the meat inside the container when the sound of James's voice made her freeze.

"I believe those were about to be served to the Winchesters."

Startled, she whipped around, giving him a look of wild alarm.

"If you really need to eat," he continued cordially, "then perhaps you'll join me. I'd be more than happy to have the waiter bring you a fresh cut. That is, if he ever gets back from iceberg-watching along with the cook, the steward, and the maître d'."

She thought that over for a second, looked at the steaks she was holding, looked back at James, and quickly placed the steaks in the container, which she then deposited inside the sack.

James shrugged. "I see you are determined to pilfer."

She nodded her head only once, quite determined. She obviously knew exactly what she was doing, and despite her elfin demeanor, James could sense a quick wit and a firm intelligence.

"Nothing I say can make you change your mind?"

She shook her head. He could have sworn she was daring him to challenge her.

James had never seen anything like it; he was very amused. "Well, in that case, may I at least assist you in selecting the best this restaurant has to offer? I've been eating here every night since we left Southampton, and I can assure you, I'm quite familiar with the menu."

She gazed at him steadily, apparently willing to trust him, and something inside of him moved. It was a small something, but it was the first tender, outgoing feeling he'd had since beginning this trip. He stared at her, wondering at her power. For some reason her height had an effect on him. It was definitely an attractive aspect of her, if only because there was so little of her; her presence seemed to light up the room. Her hair floating around her head gave her the appearance of a sprite. He still hadn't heard her voice, and suddenly he wanted to hear it as much as he wanted her to stay.

His scrutiny of her must have been more intense than he realized, because she drew back slowly, her eyes shifting toward her only getaway, the window.

James caught her eyes and also glanced at the window, noting that she would have to get past him if she wanted to reach it.

"Why do I have the feeling you don't want anyone to know you're here?" He studied her closely, stroking his chin, as she continued to inch away.

"You're not a stowaway, are you?"

The look of absolute guilt on her face confirmed it.

"Aha, so that's it, he said, wagging a finger at her. "You *are* a stowaway, aren't you?"

She tried to ignore him, turning directly toward the window.

"You know they'll put you in the brig if they catch you," he said with a smile. "It would be a shame to have such a charming—uh—visitor in that awful prison at the bottom of the ship. I understand the roar of the ship's engines is so loud down there that it can drive a person insane."

That did it. Suddenly she sprang forward across the room, making a beeline for the window. And if not for his quick reflexes, she would have escaped. Still, stopping her wasn't going to be all that easy. In the end he wished she had gotten away from him, considering the fight she put up.

She struggled frantically, hell-bent on escape. As he held her tightly around the waist, she kicked, gripping the window ledge and fighting to climb over it. The more he held on, the harder she fought, until he wasn't sure it was worth the effort. But no amount of resistance from her was going to prevent his finding out who she was. Her determination to get away only increased his curiosity.

"Calm down!" he shouted. "I'm not going to turn you in. I promise." But it was to no avail. "Listen, whoever you are, I'm not going to hurt you."

He meant what he said, but it didn't matter, because *she* hurt *him*. In one final burst, her legs smashed into his solar plexus, rendering him momentarily helpless. He gasped and let go, clutching his abdomen and fully expecting her to disappear.

But she didn't. She stopped and stared at him, resplendent and doubled over in his tuxedo, and suddenly she burst out laughing.

James reached for the nearest glass and took a long swallow. "So you think that's funny, do you?" he asked in murderous tones. "Obviously I underestimated your abilities."

Her laughter had a magical quality, tinkling like the high keys of a piano. But he was no longer in the mood for magic. This little elf was a force to be reckoned with; and, fueled by anger, he picked up a bottle of champagne and advanced toward her, with the idea of dousing the top of her bewitching little head.

But she misread his intentions. As he stood over her, still panting from exertion, she held up both hands in abject fear, the look of terror on her face telling him that she thought he was about to clobber her with the bottle.

He looked sideways at the bottle in his hand and then back at her. "You didn't really think I was going to bash you with this, did you?"

She nodded frantically, looking suddenly like a small child.

"That is ridiculous," he said with crushing dignity. "Do you really think I'd waste this good bottle of Dom Perignon on your cranium?"

He lowered the bottle, and she didn't move. Perhaps she was beginning to trust him, just a little. James felt as if he had gotten hold of a cyclone. He reached out and tentatively touched her shoulder. It was slight but sturdy, and he had the idea that she might take off again or disappear into a cloud of smoke, but she didn't flinch. Capturing her blue eyes with an unspoken challenge, he let his hand slide down her arm until it reached her hand. It was soft and small, and the fingers curled suddenly around his. Instantly, his face lit up in a smile of great triumph, as though he had just won the Olympics.

"There now, that's better," he said. "Why don't we

start at the beginning? My name is James William Bentley."

She blinked, and he could have sworn she looked skeptical. No one ever looked askance at James William Bentley, but right now he was more curious about her.

"You do have a name, don't you?"

"Maybe."

Now he was surprised. "Ah, so you do speak."

"When the need arises." Her voice was light and silvery, like a small bell.

James pressed her gently. "And what is your name?"

She seemed to be thinking this over. After looking up at the ceiling and then down at her feet, her eyes finally rested on his. "Chastity."

James stifled a laugh. "Did you just make that up, or were you having trouble remembering it?"

"Both," she said. "I have many names, but for the moment, Chastity will do." She picked up a napkin and matter-of-factly wiped something from his shoulder. "A little champagne," she explained.

He took this opportunity to get a really good look at her. She was probably in her mid-twenties, although she looked a good deal younger, and there were small signs of fatigue in her face. "Hmmm, you look a little pale," he observed. "I take it that's from not eating."

"This ship rocks dreadfully at night," she confided. "I hate boats. I'm always afraid they're going to sink." She looked at him and added, "I can't swim, you know."

"Well, don't worry," James assured her. "This ship is practically unsinkable."

She gave him a baleful look. "Isn't that what they said about the *Titanic?*"

He didn't answer back, opting instead to let her continue cleaning him off.

"There you are," she smiled. "Like new."

He looked at her eyes, the most limpid color of impossible blue he had ever seen. She was truly ethereal, and altogether desirable. The realization of this hit him smoothly, and when her ripe lips parted suddenly, he knew he was going to kiss her. Maybe not now, not if she wouldn't let him, but definitely later. These things had a tendency to be inevitable, but he preferred to orchestrate them himself whenever possible. In his experience with women, which was as large as his fortune, he had learned that sometimes a direct approach was best. "May I kiss you?" he asked with suave politeness.

Chastity backed off at once, eyeing him with grave suspicion. "Why?"

"Oh, I don't know. I guess because ever since you came in here I've wondered what it would be like to kiss a pixie."

"Am I a pixie?"

He scrutinized her closely, his eyes raking down her petite form with unmistakable sensuality. "You most certainly are."

She thought it over. "What will you give me if I let you kiss me?" Her eyes were teasing, and he knew that she wasn't going to kiss him unless she damn well wanted to.

James gestured around. "All the food here that can fit into that sack of yours."

She thought that over for a few seconds, looked at

James, and then thought again. "Will you help me gather all this food?"

"It would be my pleasure," James said, "but only for a kiss."

She looked outside at the night sky. "Well, all right then, but only on the cheek." And she turned her face demurely, offering him her right cheek, but he was not to be taken lightly. Before she could stop him, he grabbed her shoulders and moved around in front of her. He kissed her directly, without any preamble, his mouth taking hers in a swift, sweet assault. Her lips were warm and tender, surprising him with a sudden jolt of intimacy. "There now," he said, more taken aback than he had expected to be. "That wasn't so bad."

But she looked decidedly unhappy. "You cheated!"

"Did I?" He knew his eyes were twinkling, but he couldn't help it.

"And I thought you were a gentleman."

James didn't answer. There was no need to. That short, sweet kiss had told him what he needed to know, and he had no doubt that there would be more, eventually. He picked up her sack and handed it to her. "We'd better hurry," he warned. He gestured to the people outside on the cold deck. "Those icebergs won't keep people occupied forever. Eventually they'll want to come back and finish their dinners." He pointed to a table near the front.

"Now, over at the Chesterfields' table are two lovely melons, which are in season. If you'll just take your sack, and—"

She shook her head airily. "I don't like honeydew."

James frowned, bemused. "Oh, I see. You don't like

honeydew melons. So beggars can be choosy, is that it?" Looking around, his eyes fell on a large bowl at the front of the room. "Fruit salad, perhaps?"

"I had that yesterday."

"So have it again today," James said, becoming irritated.

"I'm not in the mood for it twice in two days. They shouldn't repeat things."

James smiled darkly. "Perhaps tomorrow you can put in a formal complaint?"

"You know I can't." She eyed him craftily. "But you could." Giving him a friendly tap on the shoulder, she leaned closer to his ear. "Perhaps you could drop a note to the chef that you would love to have some tomato aspic."

"I'll be sure to mention it to him," James said dryly as he eyed the angle of her profile so close to his face. She was enchanting, no doubt about that. Once again a stirring of desire rose within him, but he decided to ignore it for now. "Meanwhile, can I can interest you in some shrimp salad?" He pointed at the huge iced bowl filled with hundreds of shrimp.

She didn't need to be asked twice. Making a beeline for the shrimp salad, she whipped out an empty container and filled it up, making sure to add a large dollop of sauce as well.

"So, you like shrimp. Very good. They say you can learn quite a bit about someone by what they eat." He was beginning to enjoy this. Sauntering over to a waiter's tray, he lifted the lid of a silver service dish. "Would you care for some yams?"

She shook her head. "They make me break out."

"No yams," James noted. He looked into the next bowl. "Perhaps some carrots?"

She shook her head again. "Taste too much like yams."

Her fussiness amazed him, but it challenged him at the same time. He walked to the next table and smiled. "Ah, here's something worth waiting for." There was a fresh salad of pickled beets in a large glass bowl. "Maybe a little beet salad?"

On that note she stuck her tongue out as if she were going to be sick.

"No beet salad," James concluded dryly. "Well, I can see this is not going to be an ordinary pilfering, is it?" He looked at her obstinate stance.

They were interrupted by the sudden reaction of the passengers on the deck as the first iceberg glided into view. Delighted cries, mingled with *oohs* and *ahhs,* floated in from the outside, distracting them for a moment. James glanced at all the transfixed people and reassured her: "Well, at least that will keep them from spoiling our little looting party, won't it?"

She folded her arms and waited for him with the same stubborn expression. Obviously she didn't like his teasing. She seemed to think that stealing food was a perfectly justified occupation and that he had no right to make fun of her.

"Forgive me," he said with an exaggerated bow, "but my innate sense of morality caught up with me for a moment. Don't worry. It's gone now." She lifted one golden eyebrow, waiting for him to finish. "Now, let's see what we have here. Ah, here we go." He gave her a sidelong glance, sure she would approve of his latest selection. "How about blueberry pie?"

She shook her head, and sighed. "I'm disappointed in you, James William," she said. "I need things that will keep for as long as possible. I can't be bothered with messy, unnecessary things like blueberry pie. I'm also in a hurry." She strode past him, looking quickly from table to table. Then her eyes caught sight of something and she was off and running. A loaf of bread, a tomato, a bunch of oranges, two baked potatoes—all of these disappeared into the depths of her sack until it began to bulge.

"Where will you put it all?" James asked her as she scooted by. "I must say, that sack of yours probably weighs more than you do by now."

She stopped and lifted it up to test it. "Perhaps you're right." Her eyes roamed around once more, and at last she darted back to the dessert cart and went for the blueberry pie. "Might as well go in for some dessert," she announced, scooping it up and securing it in plastic wrap.

James watched her, amused. "Don't forget the champagne," he said, pouring some into a glass. "What good are those luscious steaks without a proper vintage?"

Instead of the glass, she opted for the entire bottle, which she pulled out of his hand.

"Perhaps you'd like to join me in a toast to—"

His words stopped abruptly as he watched her drink lustily straight out of the bottle. She closed her eyes for a moment in satisfaction, and it occurred to him that she must have eaten very little in days. When she tried to replace the bottle on the table, he stopped her.

"Keep it," he insisted. "Please."

She placed it back on the table anyway, and let her eyes roam around the room with the predatory squint he was becoming accustomed to. A second later she was scooping up an unopened bottle of champagne from an ice bucket.

"Of course," he said. "How silly of me. Why not get a fresh one?"

He leaned over to explore the floral centerpiece on his table. After a moment, he decided on the yellow rose. It took a moment before he was able to retrieve it.

"Here you are," he said, turning to present her with it. But when he looked up, she wasn't there. Startled, he looked wildly around the room, but she had vanished. The yellow rose dangled from his fingers as he stood there, feeling suddenly very foolish.

CHAPTER
Two

"YOU'RE MISSING A BEAUTIFUL sighting, my boy."

His uncle's voice hailed him from the double French doors that led to the deck, but he didn't respond. He wanted to savor this last moment of precious solitude that had been so delightfully broken by his mercurial pixie.

"A triple sighting, James. If you hurry, you can still catch a glimpse of it." His uncle, Henry Jamison, a dapper, silver-haired man in his sixties, crossed the large room and hovered over him. "Imagine, three icebergs, each the size of a mountain, floating in the ocean!"

James looked up from the rose. "If I wanted to see floating ice, Uncle, I would have ordered a martini on the rocks, instead of this overpriced soda water they try to pass off as champagne." He gestured to the bottle and smiled at his own hypocrisy. Only moments before he had nothing but praise for it.

His uncle looked at him strangely. "That soda water you so sarcastically refer to is a Dom Perignon Forty-nine, if I'm not mistaken. It's one of the finest vintages I've ever tasted. And as for the price, we both know you would never go into debt even if you overindulged in it for the next thousand years."

James broke in with a weary sigh. "Maybe not, but it certainly hadn't been doing much to perk me up."

"Aha, so now we have the real culprit—boredom."

James shifted impatiently. He, James William Bentley, with his lively, active mind, could never be bored. "Whatever do you mean?" he asked crossly.

"The disease of the upper class. It generally strikes between the ages of twenty-seven to thirty-two."

"I am thirty," James acknowledged dryly. "And I suppose you're right. I *am* bored, although I can't imagine why. It's just a phase, no doubt. It will pass."

"Well, I know it's not your job, dear nephew. Being the chairman of the board of Bentley Industries is the best it gets."

"Exactly. Where do I go from here?" James pointed out.

Henry Bentley pondered that for a moment and then raised a finger. "You have all the money you'll ever need."

"Little incentive for making more," James countered.

"You could travel the world again."

James gestured around him. "What do you think I'm doing on this ship?"

The question was interrupted by two young men who

came bursting through the doors. One was dressed in the requisite black tie and was stumbling slightly, a glazed smile plastered across his face. He held a bottle in one hand and a glass in the other. The other young man had gold-rimmed glasses and a head of wiry hair. The only first-class passenger not decked out in black tie, he was wearing a fitted black jumpsuit, a white shirt with flowing sleeves, a black string tie, and a billowing black cape.

"Hey, James, old boy," the tipsy one said. "You should see those icebergs. It will make your whole trip worthwhile." He looked at his friend. "Go on, tell him, Zeebo."

Zeebo Molinari was an outrageously successful agent for promising young artists, many of whom had already gained national recognition under his guidance. He delighted in doing whatever was least expected of him, and cheerfully admitted to anyone who asked that his snooty demeanor was mostly an affectation. He gave his inebriated friend a withering look before addressing James. "What Oliver here is trying to say is that there appears to be an iceberg with three peaks protruding above the water line, giving the illusion of three separate mountains of ice. As to whether or not this makes your whole trip worthwhile is another matter entirely."

James shrugged. "Couldn't hurt." And with a careless smile that hid his sudden stab of wistfulness, he sniffed the flower again, tore off the stem, and placed the rose into his empty buttonhole. The others were all trooping out to the deck, and after a moment he decided to follow them. "See you later," he called to his uncle. Maybe—what had she called herself? Chastity. Not her real name, no doubt. Then again, with her, he couldn't be sure. Anyway, maybe that was where she had disappeared to.

He positioned himself at the rail facing toward the stern, looking around to see if she was there. She wasn't. He looked up just in time to witness three magnificent peaks of ice receding in the wake of the ship. They had a majestic, ghostly aura in the moonlight that commanded even his attention. They were a silent, magnificent reminder that the world was shaped by forces other than his own. Still, his mind was elsewhere as he thought back to the bold kiss he had given his errant little pixie. His determination hardened. She had to be somewhere on this ship, and he would find her. Soon.

He looked down to the second-class deck below. Perhaps stowing away in one of the lifeboats? Or had she been lucky enough to find an empty cabin nearby?

"A pretty sight," James murmured as the last of the icebergs receded from view.

"There'll be more, James, old boy," Oliver said, giving him an outsized slap on the back.

"Not like this one. She was—" He stopped talking and looked at his friends.

Zeebo sized him up and shook his head ruefully. "It appears that our friend here is not talking about floating ice. Are you, James?"

James only smiled.

"He's not talking at all," Oliver said. "But I've got a feeling it's about a woman."

"Brilliant, Oliver. You have such a way of wheedling answers out of people. You really should go to law school." Zeebo smiled at James. "The icebergs have gone. The fun seems to be over, and the people are all retreating back to the dining room. Now if you'll excuse me, I shall follow suit. But first I must go to the storage vaults and inspect my property. The pitch of the ship may have shifted them somewhat."

"What, again?" Oliver asked, peeved. "That will be the third time tonight." He turned to James and added, "You'd think he was carrying all the crown jewels of Europe instead of a handful of valuable—"

Zeebo shook him vigorously, and snatched the bottle from his wavering hand. "I think you've had enough to drink, my friend. Shall I escort you to your cabin? We wouldn't want you to slip and fall overboard, now, would we?" He gave Oliver a warning stare, and Oliver staggered backward in confusion.

"Sorry," he apologized, "no harm intended."

"That's all right, Zeebo," James said as he glanced casually around the area. Crowds of people were moving back inside, and he was able to see more faces than before. "I had a sneaking suspicion already. But don't worry. Your treasures are safe. I won't tell a soul."

Zeebo looked at him oddly. "I have a legitimate fear, you know. After all, there have already been thefts reported aboard this ship. Might I remind you of the Winchesters? The thieves took mostly jewelry and available cash, but they'll probably take whatever they can."

Oliver shook his head angrily. "This is the first time I've ever heard of such a thing happening on board a luxury liner. Imagine the boldness of those people, whoever they are."

Suddenly James saw her. His face dropped in surprise at how casually she walked along the dimly lit deck, the moonlight casting dancing shadows through her hair.

"Are you all right, James?"

"That's her," he said as he watched the young woman walk as quietly as an Indian along the dark side of the ship. She was looking around cautiously, first on this deck and then down the side of the ship. A thick rope wound over her shoulder, and as he watched, she placed the bag of food over the side of the railing.

"Who are you looking at?" Oliver asked.

"My little pixie." He struggled to see her in the dark. Either he was imagining it or she had attached the rope to the railing and was about to climb over it. The next few seconds confirmed his suspicions. "My God, she's going to jump!"

Passengers within the sound of his voice looked around in alarm and then at each other.

Zeebo looked also, but saw nothing. "Where?" he asked nervously. "I can't see a thing in this light."

He was right: It was too dark to see; but, knowing that a fall would send her drowning in the ocean, James broke away, shouting for her to stop. "Don't do it!" he called. But it was too late. In another moment she was gone. He crashed into the railing and looked down at the ocean passing by in endless white breakers off the ship's hull. "Chastity!" he called down.

Passengers gathered around him, and Zeebo and Oliver peered with him into the water. The purser flew past everyone to get to James.

"Man overboard, sir?"

James looked at him. "I'm not sure." He thought it

over quickly and then changed his mind. "Yes, man overboard."

That was enough. The purser ran to get help and a few seconds later the ship had halted and lifeboats were lowered. Everyone was out on the decks now, looking around.

The ocean was flooded with lights, seamen with binoculars swarmed around the deck, and lifeboats crisscrossed through the water as poor James stood at the railing straining his eyes and hoping this was all a false alarm.

But there was no way to know. By now all the passengers had come back out to watch the search, hoping along with James that someone could be found. Yet James hoped he was wrong about her falling in. In the end, no sign of a mishap could be found, and the captain called off the search. It was past one o'clock in the morning and the three were right back where they had started.

"Well, James," Zeebo said as he patted James's back. "I'm sure this was just a false alarm."

"Yes," said Oliver. "That's all it is. Why not join us for a nightcap?"

James waved them off as he watched the lifeboats being drawn up. "I think I'll stay till the very end," he said. "You never can tell."

His friends walked off, leaving him leaning against the railing. If she hadn't fallen in, she had to be hiding somewhere on this ship, enjoying the meal they had put together.

"Where are you, you mysterious woman?" He leaned against the railing, which accidentally caught the band of his gold watch. "Oh, no!" he cried, but it was too late. He watched in despair as his watch fell from his wrist to the deck below.

Susan Melinka snuggled back against the canvas that surrounded her hiding place, content in her ingenuity and her safety. True, it wasn't the Ritz, but it would hold her well enough until they reached their destination, and that was all she cared about. During the day she was free to roam about the ship and avail herself of its amenities. No one had questioned her, and her confidence had grown as the voyage progressed.

She was neatly sheltered in a large stretch of canvas that was attached to the back of the ship, fanning out over a large wooden board that served as a makeshift floor. The canvas was secured to the stern with metal rings that hooked onto ropes, and so far it had held up beautifully. True, one person had seen her and she knew he would recognize her if he saw her again. She certainly wasn't likely to forget the tawny eyes that had scrutinized her with such raw sensuality. And he had had a certain elegance, a certain sense of restraint that was wildly attractive. If he hadn't turned her in by now, she was sure he would keep her secret.

Her hideaway was furnished with a blanket; her suitcase, which functioned as a table; a candle; and the sack of food that James William Bentley had helped her to fill. It was all she needed. She had been traveling around Europe on a shoestring for two years now, and she had made do with accommodations even more primitive than this.

Although she didn't like the idea of stowing away,

she had finally run out of money last month, and the only thing to do was return home. She had managed to scrape by for two years, singing with a folk group in a tavern in Scotland for one summer, working as a bartender in a tiny town in Greece (even though she spoke no Greek), and joining the huge flow of migrant workers who came up from Spain for the grape harvest in France every autumn. She had asked for a shipboard job to pay her passage, but had been curtly turned away. Stung by the refusal and expert at crafty survival solutions by now, Susan had found her own clandestine way to cross the ocean.

She hadn't planned on traveling for two years. It had just happened. All Susan knew when she had started out was that she had to get away, to expand her horizons, to escape from the knowledge that Jeffrey Duncan no longer wanted to marry her.

Jeffrey had been her childhood sweetheart, her pal, and, she had believed with all her heart, her soulmate. They had shared everything since they were in the second grade, and she had grown up in the comfortable knowledge that, for her, the universal search for love was over.

The world had never been bigger to her than her hometown of Method, Idaho, and until two years ago, she had had no need for it to be. When Jeffrey had sat her down and told her it was over, he might as well have told her that her life was over. She had withdrawn in her room like a widow for a month, losing fifteen pounds and refusing all visitors. At the end of the month she had gone to the travel agent in Fernwood and bought a one-way ticket to Helsinki, which was the most outlandish place she could think of. The shock of a foreign country had been the tonic she needed, and although it had taken a long time for the wound to heal, she had slowly been gaining confidence and a newfound optimism ever since.

It was now very late, and the constant shuffle of people on the deck had finally settled down. There had been some commotion earlier, something about a man overboard, and she had burrowed deep into her canvas for the better part of an hour to avoid discovery. Now, however, everything was quiet again. She lit her candle and took a deep breath of the fresh ocean air, sheltering the small flame with her hands.

Suddenly she heard footsteps up on the deck. She hesitated and then relaxed. A late-night stroller, no doubt. Nothing to be concerned about. No one would be able to see her unless they happened to peer inside the circle of canvas at the ship's stern, and there was nothing about the canvas that looked very interesting.

The footsteps stopped nearby, and she muffled a laugh as someone above her began to talk out loud.

"It's actually lost," a man's voice said. "I don't believe it."

There was something very familiar about that voice, and she resisted the urge to peek outside. "I've been looking for an hour. I'm not going to find it," the voice grumbled, and suddenly she knew who it was. She had met only one person on board this ship. It could only be her fellow pilferer, James William Bentley.

"Hey, down there!" he called out. She almost jumped. Could he possibly be talking to her? "Hey, fish!" he continued. "Have any of you seen a gold watch? I'll give you a nice reward for it." Susan's eyes widened as she listened. He wasn't talking to her, he was talking to the fish. And he was offering a reward for a gold watch. Her heart began to beat faster.

"That's it," he continued seriously. "I'll offer a reward to whoever finds my watch." He began laughing at himself. "What should the reward be for a ten-thousand-dollar gold-and-diamond watch?"

He seemed to be thinking this over for quite a while until he came up with the answer.

"Twenty percent," he announced. "Two thousand dollars to the one who returns it." He leaned over the railing and called giddily, "That goes for you too, fish! That kind of money can buy a lot of worms or whatever it is you might eat besides my watch."

Susan looked at the watch in her hand. It had fallen from heaven right through her canvas hiding place and into the blueberry pie. "So this is worth ten thousand, huh?" she said. She thought about the reward money he had offered the fish, and made up her mind fast. She still didn't want to risk being seen—but for two thousand dollars she could let him know she was there.

Very carefully, she lifted one hand above the railing and waved it back and forth. She could tell that he saw it, because she heard a sudden intake of breath and a slight movement as he came closer. His monologue came to a halt as she continued to wave her hand until she was positive she had his undivided attention.

"What the devil—" she heard him mutter. She smiled.

Letting her hand fall gracefully forward from the wrist and turning it palm-side up, she crooked her index finger and beckoned with as much mystery and drama as she could muster. She knew that all he could see was her hand, with its steadily beckoning finger, and she wondered if he would heed her summons.

She didn't have to wait long. He strode right over to the rail, his footsteps decidedly impatient, and peered down into the darkness. His face was full of questioning suspicion, but it changed the moment he saw her.

"It's you!" he exclaimed with an odd combination of delight and annoyance. "Again!" His eyes quickly took in her surroundings and he shook his head in disbelief. "You look like a mermaid caught in a net," he announced. "Is that it? *Are* you a mermaid?"

He looked as if he half expected it to be true, but she didn't bother to answer. She smiled engagingly as he looked more closely at her setup, blanching slightly as he realized how precarious her perch was. The canvas was secured by hooks and ropes, but it hung right over the water.

"Are you all right in there?" he croaked.

"Certainly," she answered graciously. She was standing in the middle of the tentlike contraption, in the roomiest part, easily keeping her balance as the ship cruised along.

He looked down past her into the canvas sheet and saw the candle burning, and the sack of food they had collected earlier.

"Is that where you hide out?"

She nodded, obviously very pleased with herself.

He looked more closely, taking in her scant possessions, and shook his head. "How is it in there?"

"Warm now, freezing at night."

He repressed a shudder. "Your arrangement is not for the faint of heart," he concluded. "You don't have a lot of room in there, do you? I'd say it's only about ten feet all around." He pulled slightly on the rigging, and the whole canvas shook.

"Hey," she warned. "Be careful. You don't want to spill an expensive bottle of champagne."

He peered down inside again. The champagne bottle was wobbling from his shaking, and the entire apparatus was altogether too precarious for his taste. "This is no place for a person to stay," James said. "It's too dangerous. What if the ropes broke and you fell in?"

She gave him a smug little smile. "I'd have to swim."

"Very funny," James said. "But surely you could have afforded some accommodation? Anything would be better than this."

"I can afford it now," she said. "I'm about to receive two thousand dollars."

"I beg your pardon?"

"The reward money—for this." She held up a gleaming object and dangled it under his nose.

"My watch!" he cried, reaching out to take it. But Susan was careful to keep it just out of his grasp. She quickly lowered it out of sight and faced him warily. "It fell right on my head in the middle of my dinner."

"Oh . . . shall I apologize?"

Her eyes twinkled. "No. But you can do even better. Don't you remember? Twenty percent?"

James cringed, but then he nodded. "Obviously, you were eavesdropping on my thinking."

"You think out loud, which is very convenient." She

gave him another smile. "So, do I get my reward?"

He was silent.

"Well," she pressed, "do I?"

"I'm thinking about it," he said.

"Well, think out loud again, okay?" she asked with a small pout. "It's easier that way."

"You know," he said, "if I hadn't opened my big mouth, you wouldn't have known about the reward."

"I also wouldn't have known that the watch was your property. Then it would have been 'finders, keepers.' Which it still is."

His eyes flashed. "Now you are going a bit far."

"All the way to New York," she agreed, "and with your watch." She examined it carefully, her dainty fingers passing over the diamond chips. "All that money just for a stupid watch. It would take me a whole year to earn what this watch cost, do you know that?" She looked up at him. "How do I know this is yours?"

James suddenly lost his patience. "Come on now, hand it over immediately. I've had enough of this."

A flash of anger went through her. "Oh, have you?" she asked haughtily. "Well, thank you, but I'd rather not hand it over just yet." She looked him up and down. "In fact," she went on, deliberately waving the watch out over the water, "I had better think this whole thing over. After all, there is a thief on board this ship. How do I know it's not you?"

He was beside himself. "Why, you little imp! How dare you? You must have taken over a hundred dollars' worth of food from the dining room, not to mention an expensive bottle of champagne. And you call me a thief?"

"I was hungry," she said simply, as if anyone should have known. "Necessity justified my actions."

"And is it necessary to know the time?" He tried swiping for the watch, but she was too quick for him.

"Oh, no, you don't." She pulled her hand back, but she miscalculated. Her balance wavered, causing her to lose her grip. She let out a small, helpless scream, waving her arms frantically.

James made a lunge for her, wrapping his arms around her body in a desperate attempt to keep her from falling into the ocean. "I've got you," he gasped as he nearly bent over the railing. He looked past her to the ocean that was flowing by underneath, and groaned. "Oh, no," he said. "I can't take much more of this."

"Well, I'm fine," she said, struggling back to her feet. "Let go of me." She looked at him oddly. What was the matter with him?

James began to straighten up, but he still held on to her. When at last he had regained his footing, she found herself looking right into his eyes, which was a most pleasant experience, but rather awkward in this position. His eyes were tawny and intelligent, as if he could learn everything about her just by looking at her; and although the sensation was unsettling, it was also appealing. "You can let go of me now," she said after too long a moment had passed. "I'm safe."

"Yes, you are, but am I?" He managed a weak smile as he let his arms drop, but he didn't let them drop far. His hands fell right into hers.

"I'm fine," she insisted gently. "Really. I happen to be an expert climber."

"Of that I have no doubt," he said wryly, regaining

his composure, "but still, one of us does need some hand-holding."

"You're not afraid of the water, are you?" she asked. It didn't seem possible. He didn't seem to be the type who was afraid of anything.

"No. Actually, it's the height that bothers me. Especially," he added with a sickened glance into the water, "when the height happens to be moving." He looked up again. "Just tell me one thing. How did you manage to get onto the first-class deck from here?" He gestured behind him. "There is a metal gate and a guard blocking all the other passengers from reaching the upper deck."

She gave him a knowing, satisfied grin. She knew she could trust him now, and she didn't mind showing off her cleverness. Reaching back down into her bag, she came up with a rope with a hook on the end. "I wasn't kidding," she said. "I'm an experienced mountain climber. With everyone engrossed in watching the icebergs, it was a great opportunity to sneak up for some first-class food." She sighed. "A good thing, too. I was getting awfully sick of hamburgers and french fries."

"Is that all they feed you down there?"

She laughed. "No, but it was the easiest thing to steal."

He stared at her for a moment, and then he burst out laughing along with her. She felt suddenly expansive, and gestured grandly to her meager surroundings. "Would you care to join me for a late-night snack?"

James looked pained. "You mean—down there?"

"Of course."

"Uh, no . . . no thanks." He tried to back away, but

she grabbed his hands and held them tightly. They were strong hands, well cared for and smooth, but strong nonetheless. She liked holding on to them, even though he looked as if he would rather be anywhere else.

"Come on, now," she said, pulling gently. "You can't keep leaning over the side like that. It's too dangerous."

"No, thank you. Really, I'd rather watch from here."

"Don't tell me you're afraid!"

"All right, I won't, but just the same, I prefer a good solid deck under my feet."

She was actually disappointed, which was absurd, considering that she was asking him to climb right off the ship, but she couldn't help it. "And nothing I do can coax you down here?"

James looked down one more time, swallowed hard, and shook his head. "Nothing."

CHAPTER
Three

A FEW MINUTES LATER, after two false starts, he had valiantly managed to hop over the railing and slide feet-first into her hideaway. She beamed at him across the small flame from the candle, which was their only source of light, and offered him a glass of champagne, which he accepted at once.

As he sipped, she took the opportunity to study him more closely. His face was undeniably aristocratic, stamped with a refinement of character that could only have been inbred. And yet it was an asymmetrical face, with strong bones and sharp features. His nose was aquiline and his cheekbones were harsh, but the total effect was one of potent masculinity and authority. His sandy hair was impeccably cut, but just now it fell over his lean forehead in careless dishevelment. She poured him another glass of champagne, which he sipped with a patrician air.

"Feeling better?" she asked.

James arched an eyebrow. "As well as possible under the circumstances. I just happen to have this slight fear of drowning when I'm hanging off-balance over the ocean."

"You're not afraid of the water, are you?"

"No." He seemed to be barely controlling his patience. "As a matter of fact, I'm an ace swimmer."

She asked, confused, "You are? Then why be afraid of drowning?"

He sighed heavily and sipped more champagne. "It's just that it's rather inconvenient to fall from a ship in one's evening clothes in the middle of the night. Other than that, no problem."

"Oh," she said, cowed.

"However, I do have a problem with heights, if that helps," he added. "I was on the swimming team in college and placed second in the finals, but there was one aspect of the sport I could never attempt." He paused, as much for drama as for reluctance to reveal the answer.

Susan leaned forward, waiting to capture his confidence.

He leaned forward also, and their faces were only inches apart. "High diving," he confessed. "I couldn't even consider it." He shuddered. "Just thinking about it gives me the creeps."

"I see," she said, nodding. "No wonder my little stunt upset you." She patted his hand. "Well, don't worry. You won't fall off. And if you do, I'll scream for help while you exercise some of that top-notch swimming." She gave him a bright smile, which he met by groaning and slapping his hand to his head.

"Thanks. I'll remember that."

There was a momentary silence during which he gulped down another glass of champagne. "Would you like something to eat?" she asked.

"Yes, pickled beets."

She smiled again. "You know I don't have any of that, James." It was the first time she had said his name, and she found that she liked it. Not Jim, but James. It had a pleasantly civilized ring to it. "James," she repeated softly, and he looked up.

"I was just testing out saying your name. James William Bentley," she said in a little singsong.

He looked amused. "Do you like my name?"

"It sounds rather splendid. As if it should have a numeral at the end of it." She gave him a mischievous glance. "You're not an English lord or anything like that, are you?"

This time he didn't look quite so amused. "My mother does happen to be Lady Constance Bentley. Her father is the seventh Earl of Lyte."

Susan gaped. "Wow! Does that make you an earl?"

"No. My cousin Henry will be the eighth earl when the time comes. I'm just a regular American citizen. My father is an American, and he has no claim to a title." He recited all this politely but mechanically, as if he had been compelled to say it many times before.

Susan watched him, pensively biting her index finger. "And you're not happy," she concluded quietly.

"What! Why would you say that? Of course I'm happy!"

She gave him an odd little grin. "No, you are not." She picked up the bottle and handed it to him. "Here, have the rest of the champagne."

He splashed some into his glass and drank. "Oh, dear, I'm getting as tipsy as Oliver."

"Careful, you have to climb back up later on . . . your lordship."

He gave her a terribly crushing look. "*Please*. That wasn't necessary . . . Chastity."

It was her turn to wince. "That's not my real name," she confessed.

"Really?" he asked with exaggerated surprise. "Well, well, you could have fooled me. Are you going to reveal the truth—or must I drag it out of you?"

She studied him for a moment. "It's Susan."

"Susan . . . well, that sounds plausible."

"Just plain old Susan Melinka. A plain all-American kid—just like you." She emptied the last drops of champagne into his glass.

"You're not trying to get me drunk, are you?" he asked, readily downing the sparkling wine. "Trying to ply me with liquor and then having your way with me?"

"Oh, no"—she giggled—"just tipsy." She reached over impulsively and pulled his undone bow tie from around his neck, looping it playfully around her own.

"It becomes you," he said with an approving nod.

"And your open collar becomes you," she answered, trying not to stare at the patch of tanned, lean chest that showed through his loosened shirt. "Do you people always go around at night in a tuxedo?"

"Only in places like this," he said, pointing to the top deck.

She shook her head. "It seems so silly. Everyone dressed up like penguins, just to eat dinner."

He eyed her quizzically. "No sillier than camping out here in this contraption, with pilfered food and no ticket."

"True," she conceded. "But at least I'm free."

He groaned. "Oh, no. Please don't regale me with any latter-day hippie philosophy. It's too late at night, and I'm definitely not in the mood."

She threw him a knowing little glance. "Don't protest too much," she warned teasingly.

"It so happens that I am every bit as 'free' as you are. More so, in fact. I just prefer different things."

Susan was vastly amused. "How can you possibly know what you prefer? You've never had the chance to find out."

"Neither have you." He regarded her silently, lifting his glass in a sardonic toast.

Susan pondered his statement, watching him out of the corner of her eye. He was so smashingly elegant that he seemed to be something out of a different age. And yet she knew she was right about one thing—the discontent she had sensed lurking behind his flawless facade.

"Maybe not," she answered slowly, "but I have tried."

He looked skeptical. "How?"

"I've been traveling all over Europe, for one thing."

"On a shoestring, obviously. Camping out and hitching rides?"

She nodded enthusiastically. "More or less. And you can't imagine how much I've learned—not just about the world, but about myself."

"Yes, I can," he said with that same world-weary grin. "I've been all over Europe, too. Just because I did it with more money doesn't mean that I learned any less. It simply means that I may have learned different things."

Susan frowned a little, unsettled, while he watched her with his knowing smile. She was used to people being impressed with her ingenuity and her travels. He was the first person she had ever met who challenged her originality. She decided to challenge his.

"Are you trying to tell me that a properly bred preppie is as street-smart and capable as someone who has had to use her wits to survive?"

"I certainly am. What gave you the patent on resourcefulness?"

She opened her arms wide and giggled, relenting. "Life!"

"Really. It so happens my father would admire your resourcefulness." He paused. "And so do I."

She looked at him. He meant it. "Thank you" was all she could say. "Tell me about your father."

He smiled. "He's a self-made man. He likes independence and stubbornness."

"He's also very rich," she said.

"Yes." He swallowed the last of the champagne.

"Tell me how your father met your mother."

He looked surprised but answered readily, "It was a practical romance. My father was in love with my mother, and my mother was in love with his money."

Susan was shocked that he could speak so matter-of-factly about it. "That's terrible!" He shrugged. "Isn't it?"

"Why?" James leaned forward and took Susan's hand. "She was a titled lady with no money. She offered him entrée along with her respect and gratitude, and he gave her the means to maintain the standard of living she wanted. It was a successful match."

"But—but didn't she fall in love with him after a while?"

"You're a hopeless romantic, Susan." His flinty voice caressed her name, and she stifled an unbidden little shiver. "My parents have an . . . arrangement. They each do what they like, and neither questions the other. It's a most civilized arrangement, and it suits both of them."

"I see." She looked out to sea for a moment, wondering what it was like to be James William Bentley, the son of a practical alliance. She couldn't imagine it, and she decided to change the subject. "I'm afraid there's no more champagne."

"It's all right. I probably drank too much anyway. And it's time I was getting back to my cabin." He stood up and immediately fell back down again, unsteady on the flimsy surface.

"Are you sure you're ready to leave here in this condition?" she asked. "Remember, you're not in the mood for a midnight swim." She reached for her sleeping bag. "You can stay here if you like. It's really quite safe."

"Are you mad?" he asked. "I couldn't possibly—"

She laughed, a tinkling sound that stopped him cold. "Are you afraid?" she taunted. "I am actually going to allow you to share my meager but very unique accommodations. It's the chance of a lifetime."

"How nice of you," he said dryly.

"On one condition," she added, holding up a finger.

A moment of tension passed between them as they eyed each other. "Please," he added, waving his hand disdainfully. "I do not need to be lectured about my manners. If I were to make an advance toward you it would be under much more respectable conditions."

"I beg your pardon?" she said.

He looked impatient. "I take it you are asking me to share your bed?"

"I am asking no such thing!" she cried, feeling suddenly foolish. She *had* asked him to stay. What was he supposed to think? "I'm sorry if I gave you the wrong impression," she added stiffly. "It's just that you do look bushed, and you may not be in the mood to climb back up onto the ship."

He cast a glance upward and looked away quickly. "Well, you're right about that. I don't think I could manage it, not tonight."

He took off his shoes and placed them neatly on two hooks that protruded through the canvas. Then he removed his jacket, and looked doubtfully at the sleeping bag. "Will there be enough room in there for the two of us?"

"Of course not, silly," she said.

He looked around the small enclosure, and gave her a curious look. "Uh—exactly where *are* you going to sleep?"

She looked at him as if any idiot should have known, and dangled a cabin key between her fingers.

Instinctively, his hand went into his pocket, and came up as empty as the blank look on his face. "So, you're a pickpocket as well?"

She gave him an angry look. "Don't be ridiculous. It fell out of your pocket a few minutes ago."

"And you expect me to believe that?"

He was actually serious, and her temper flared, making her blue eyes flash. "If you're so sure I'm a thief, why don't you check your wallet as well?"

He thought about that for a moment, shook his head at the idea, and pulled it out with a disgruntled air. Opening the billfold, he showed it to her.

Susan gulped. "It's empty!"

"Yes," he said grimly. His eyes turned to steel as he looked at her for an explanation.

Susan began to stammer. "I—I swear to you, James, I never touched your wallet!" She looked at him beseechingly, but his face was a stony blank. "Why should I do a thing like that?"

His expression said plainly that the answer was obvious, and she began to panic. "Yes, it's true I'm broke, but I wouldn't steal!"

A cold, humorless little smile darted across his face.

"Okay, I stole food, but that's not money. Money is money. Food is food. And I can't eat money," she babbled on, and he merely watched her without saying a word. Finally she stopped and tried to think. "How much was stolen?"

He hesitated. "What do you mean?"

"How much money was taken from your wallet?"

He shrugged. "About eight English pounds—"

Susan gave him a sunburst of a smile. "Well, that's not so bad!"

"—and approximately two thousand American dollars."

She closed her eyes and tried to digest that, but all she could do was swallow several times and avoid his gaze. She had no idea what to say to him. Finally she realized that she would have to convince him. She faced him bravely and opened her arms wide. "So frisk me. Right now. Search this whole place if you like."

"This is hardly the place."

"If you believe I stole it, search me."

"I'm in no condition to do so."

"But you think I got you drunk so I could pick your pocket, right?"

"I'm hardly drunk, just tired and a little tipsy. And I haven't accused you of anything. After all, you will return my watch, won't you?"

She lit up. "And you will give me the reward?"

He looked at her as if she were crazy. "It is obvious that the reward of two thousand dollars has been stolen. But if you find it, there is a reward."

"Let me get this straight. A reward for finding the reward?"

James looked completely fed up. "We'll discuss that in the morning. Meanwhile I need my rest." He spoke with such authority that she didn't dare contradict him. He lay down carefully, adjusting the sleeping bag against the canvas. "I can't believe I'm doing this," he said. "I'm just going to try to go to sleep so that I won't have time to think about it. I hope this thing I'm in doesn't end up in the drink."

"Don't worry," she assured him, "I secured it before we left England. I'm a mountain climber, remember?"

"Yes, among other things."

She tried to think of a suitable retort, but he had already turned over. "Good night, sweet prince," she said. "When you've had enough sleep, you know where I can be found."

Throwing her climbing rope over her arm, she leaped up and out of the canvas. After making sure all was clear, she hopped over the railing and looked back down at him.

"Good night, mermaid," she heard him say.

Susan awoke the next morning with an aching back. She had had trouble the night before trying to figure out how to open the compact sofabed in James's cabin. Exhausted, she had simply opted for sleeping on it as is. But now, as she carefully unwound her cramped limbs from its narrow surface, Susan was regretting her hasty decision.

As she stood up and stretched, she had a clearheaded chance to inspect his cabin. Surprisingly, it was a very small room, no larger than the simple ten by fifteen cabins in second class. The convertible sofa allowed one to use the cabin as a sitting room during the day without the encumbrance of a bed.

She examined the two doors in the rear, figuring that one was a bathroom and the other a closet. She was about to locate the bathroom for a much-needed hot shower when there was a sudden knock at the door.

"Mr. Bentley? It's Peters, sir. I have your papers."

The doorknob rattled several times and then another knock followed.

"I have your papers, Mr. Bentley. Mr. Bentley?" A bell rang suddenly, but not in the cabin. Susan looked around wildly as she realized that it was coming from somewhere inside the closet door. It sounded like a doorbell ringing, but why would it sound inside the closet?

"I was able to get you everything you requested," Peters announced. There was a pause. "Are you there, sir?"

She could hear a set of keys jingling. The sound of a key entering a lock galvanized her into action. She couldn't risk being caught. Her only means of escape was to hide in the closet or the bathroom. Whichever door she chose would suffice, and she hurried over to the nearest one.

"The closet," she surmised, pushing some jackets aside to scrunch down in the back. She listened to the sound of Peters's entrance, then a thud, as he tossed something onto the coffee table.

"Good morning, Peters." Now James's voice was there too. He must have come in right behind Peters. She could hear him only inches from where she hid in the closet.

"Good morning, sir." Peters's voice seem to fall off a little. "Pardon my intrusion, sir, but you look as if you could use some assistance this morning. Shall I run a bath, perhaps, and call for the barber?"

"Yes, a wonderful idea—" James suddenly changed his mind. "On second thought, no."

"Very good, sir. Shall I leave your papers in this room or take them inside?"

Inside? Susan frowned. Where was inside?

"Here will be fine. Oh, and Peters . . . uh—I'm sorry I locked the outer door on you, but with all these burglaries on board, I thought it a good idea."

"You're quite right, sir. We have already informed customs in New York about it, and they will do a more than customary search of everyone's luggage in the hopes of retrieving the stolen goods."

"Which will delay us all, I suppose, but with good cause."

Susan heard a ruffling of papers.

"Ah," James said. "I see you were able to bring me a good share of reading today."

"Yes, sir. As you ordered. *The London Times, The Washington Post, The Wall Street Journal, The New York Times,* and *People* magazine."

People magazine? Susan giggled, and promptly slapped a hand over her mouth.

"Did you say something, sir?"

"Uh, no."

"Would you like your usual this morning, sir?"

"Make that double on everything," James said. "And—triple on the coffee." After a pause he added, "Delay that breakfast about an hour, will you? I'd like to clean up a bit first."

"Certainly, sir."

Susan listened as Peters left. There was a pause, then a turning of the knob on the closet door, and finally a knock.

"It's all right; it's just me. You can come out now."

She opened the door and giggled. "*People* magazine?"

He gave her a wry look and shrugged. "I like it, is that so bad?"

Susan paused, then she gave him an impish smile. "No, I guess not. Do you read the tabloids at the supermarket as well?"

"Sure," he said gamely. "When I'm in the supermarket."

That silenced her, as she realized that he probably never went to a supermarket.

Susan stepped out of the closet and looked James up and down, whistling at his disheveled condition. "You look terrible," she announced candidly.

He arched one quizzical eyebrow. "Oh, really? Perhaps if I had been allowed the comfort of my suite, I might look a little better."

He pulled off his already loosened tie and tossed it aside. "At least you had a good night's sleep." He looked at her expectantly, but she said nothing.

"Was my bed too firm for you?"

"It was okay," she said, trying to sound polite.

He rubbed a smudge of dirt from her face. "You could have at least showered before getting in it."

"Getting in it? I couldn't even open it!"

"Open it?" He looked at her face and followed her gaze, which was leveled on the couch.

"Here, *you* try it," she said as she led him over to it. She tried to pull it open again, but to no avail. "Go on, open it."

James looked at her incredulously. "Open *what?*"

"This." She gestured. "It must be broken—or else I'm just inept."

"What are you—?" He sat down abruptly on the lumpy couch, felt a worn spring, and made a sour face.

"I really think you ought to get better accommodations than this for your money," Susan said to him. "This is what the second-class cabins look like. A little smaller, but about the same way. Only they at least have a chest of drawers." She looked around again and shook her head. "Where do you put your clothes, anyway?"

"You," he said, looking at her in amazement, "are unbelievable."

"Are you talking about me?"

"Yes, you. I let you have my room for the night and you never even bothered to enter it."

CHAPTER
Four

"WHAT DO YOU MEAN by that?" Susan's head whipped around the room in confusion. Her eyes stopped as she spotted the two doors, and then it dawned on her. "Oh, no."

"Oh, yes," he said.

She continued to stare, unable to move.

"Go on," he said, giving her a nudge toward them.

With a sinking heart, she inched toward the nearest one. "It's just a closet, right?"

He grinned and shook his head.

"Oh, no. The bedroom is in here, isn't it?"

"Now there you're wrong," he said. "It is not the bedroom."

Puzzled, Susan opened the door slowly and let it swing wide to reveal a beautiful living room suite. "I'm dreaming," was all she could say.

She didn't move for several seconds as she took in her surroundings. The suite was extravagant, with plush gray velvet furnishings, a complete dining area, an oval window that provided an ample view of the ocean, a state-of-the-art stereo system, a wet bar, and a baby grand piano.

Susan felt James's hands on her elbows as he guided her farther into the room. They moved over thick gray carpeting toward a carved set of double doors, then he gestured grandly at them.

"The bedroom," he announced.

"This should be illegal," she choked out as he pushed them open to reveal a king-sized bed, a fully equipped bathroom, and two steps up, a separate sitting area with an entertainment unit and another wet bar.

James appraised her as she stared at the splendor. "Let's start with showers, shall we? We both need one. You first," he concluded generously, but she was still too stunned to move.

"This is—I could have slept *here?*" she said in a tiny little squeak. She knew she sounded like an idiot, but she didn't care.

"That's right, you blew it," James said with an amused smile. "But you can still take a shower and recoup your losses."

"All right," she mumbled, staring toward the lavish bathroom tiled in blue and green.

James sat down on the bed, and after a moment, fell back against its many pillows with a huge sigh. Susan stopped. "What's the matter?" he asked.

"Well, it's just that—are you going to stay here?" she asked.

"Of course. This is my cabin, remember?"

She was torn between modesty and gratitude and tried to phrase her next words carefully. "Uh—if you don't mind, I'd kind of like to be alone now. I mean—that is, I'm very grateful, but we've only just met, and . . . well, I need some privacy, that's all."

"Privacy?" James looked decidedly piqued. "Do you have any idea where I've been all night? I happen to be exhausted. All I wanted to do was to sack out on this bed. I'm not going to peek through the keyhole, you know."

"I know, but I'll have to get dressed and look presentable. Couldn't you just wait in the other room?"

James was regarding her through narrowed eyes. "I've got a wonderful idea. I'll go first." He jumped off the bed, strode past her into the bathroom, and slammed the door, locking it behind him.

Susan stared at the closed door and began to feel just the slightest bit ridiculous. "Humph," she said aloud, trying to restore her already wounded sense of dignity. She certainly was botching the one friendly relationship she had formed on this ship. She had trusted him, and now she was pushing him too far. And yet she couldn't let him take advantage of her. If she wasn't careful, he could turn her in, for all she knew. Her position was precarious, but she had to expect that. She was, after all, a stowaway.

She ambled around the room, wondering why she had been so insistent with him. It wasn't really modesty at all. She stopped as she heard the sound of the shower being turned on, and a sudden image of James William Bentley standing naked in the shower flashed through her mind. So that was it, she realized with a little shiver. She hadn't wanted to be vulnerable and so near him at the same time. He was a devastatingly attractive man. She would have felt too uncomfortable showering only a few feet away from him.

There were a few photographs on the dresser, and she stopped to look at them—partly out of curiosity and partly to distract her own disturbing thoughts. One was of a much younger James standing in front of what looked like a London town house with a silver-haired woman; another was of a laughing, ruddy-faced man sitting in an armchair holding a mug of beer. His parents, she surmised. It was interesting that he brought pictures of them along when he traveled. She peeked into the walk-in closet, and discovered elegant, hand-tailored clothes, all hung neatly on wooden hangers, all spread about one inch apart.

Still disturbed by her awareness of him, she went into the living room and sat at the piano, idly fingering the keys. This place was like a dream. She hadn't imagined that such places really existed. And James must think she was an absolute fool.

Lost in thought as she absently hit a few keys, Susan wondered what he could possibly want with her. Surely he had his pick of women. He was better-looking than any man had a right to be. He was interesting and stimulating and he obviously had no cause to worry about money. And—she had to face it—he excited her beyond reason. She didn't know what it was about him, but that subtle air of certainty, of power, permeated everything else about him. It made her want to challenge him and surrender to him at the same time. The thought was so confusing, so frustrating, that she struck the piano keys, creating a jarring, discordant sound that made her jump.

"You play wonderfully," James said cheerfully as he strolled into the room wrapped in nothing but a bath towel. "Beethoven, I presume?" Susan turned away from the tantalizing sight of him. "For a free spirit, you really are rather tense, do you know that?"

She whipped around to face him, amazed that he had just echoed her own thoughts. "I was just . . ." Her green eyes widened as she groped for a graceful response. When she couldn't come up with one, he gave her a devilish smile.

It was that smile, filled with sensual challenge, that galvanized her into action. "Is it my turn to use the shower?" she asked.

James bowed deeply from the waist and gestured grandly toward the door. "Of course. Be my guest." Unfortunately—and for all she knew, intentionally on his part—his towel gaped open at his movement, allowing Susan a scandalous view of bare male thigh. It was muscular, yet lean, and bronzed by the sun like the rest of his body. She swallowed hard and stood up, knowing that she would have to pass close by him in order to get through the door.

He looked up suddenly and smiled, momentarily breaking the tension. "Don't be nervous," he said gently. "I'm not going to bite. Go right ahead." How he could manage to read her mind so accurately was beyond her, but Susan gave him a shaky smile back and headed for the bathroom, stooping with affected casualness in the doorway.

"Don't be silly," she said, tossing her mane of blond curls. "I'm not nervous."

"Oh, but you are," he insisted, his clear eyes twinkling. "And I can't imagine why."

She was positive that he could. He was toying with her, and that wasn't fair. "I'm afraid that your towel is going to fall off," she blurted out, mortified the moment she had said it.

James blinked in genuine surprise, giving her a small measure of satisfaction. "Well, I'll be. You're really not such a free spirit after all, are you?"

"I was brought up to be prudent and . . . sensible."

"Aha. Treading the straight and narrow. An interesting philosophy for a stowaway."

Susan gave a world-weary sigh, suddenly worn out by the conversation. "Why don't you get dressed?" she suggested. "I'll wait out here."

"As you wish." He gave her a little salute and headed back inside while she waited. She listened unabashedly to the intimate sounds of James dressing, and then to the sound of water being turned on.

James appeared again, dressed in tan twill trousers, an oxford shirt, and recently shined brown loafers. He looked casual yet commanding, like a modern king on his day off. "Your bath has been drawn, madame."

She followed him inside, stifling a groan when she got a good look at the bathroom. "This can't be possible."

"You've never seen a bathtub before?"

"Not like this one." She stared at the tub, which was outrageously deep and wide, filled with luxurious bubbles adorned with brass fixtures and knobs marked

"HOT," "COLD," and "TEPID." On an ornate side table lay a selection of scented bath gels, a hair dryer, spare toothbrushes, a variety of soaps and shampoos, an extra oversized bathrobe, huge, fluffy towels, and a separate dressing area with a vanity and a full-length mirror.

As soon as James left, closing the door behind him, Susan lost no time in shedding her clothes and sinking into the inviting bubbles. She breathed a long, deep sigh of relief as the hot, sudsy water enveloped her tired body, soothing her frazzled nerves.

Before long she was singing lazily to herself, lifting one slender leg high in the air and watching an army of tiny bubbles slide downward as she warbled an offkey version of "If They Could See Me Now."

Her voice drifted out to James, who was thumbing through a pile of newspapers without seeing them, trying to keep his mind off the pixie who was casting a spell on his bathroom. He didn't pretend to understand her for a moment, but he was getting used to that. One minute she was practically inviting him into bed, and the next she displayed the modesty of a nun. It didn't make sense, but he intended to get to the bottom of it. A restless longing stirred within him as he thought of her lounging in his tub, and he glanced automatically at his wrist to check the time before realizing that she still had his watch.

"Hey, in there," he called after forty minutes had passed. "You've been in there an awfully long time. You'll turn into a prune." He headed back into the bedroom and waited for her to end her song. She didn't answer, and after another five minutes James grew impatient. He got up and went to the door of the bathroom, giving it one sharp rap. "Hey, in there."

"Hey, yourself."

"Are you all right?" He turned the handle of the door, intending only to rattle it for emphasis, and was surprised to find that it was unlocked and opened easily.

"That's far enough, mister," she said at once, her gentle voice trying to sound stern and very nearly succeeding.

The door was only open three inches, but he caught a glimpse of her clothes piled on the chair by the door. The mirror was a bit steamy, but it reflected the hazy outline of her body as she lay in the tub, the bubbles long since melted away.

"Don't you dare come in here," she commanded, sounding more worried than authoritative.

James knew he should close the door again, but he was too mesmerized by the sight of her slight, ethereal form. Loose strands of golden hair floated lazily in the water, and one small foot was draped over the side of the tub, a pool of water forming slowly beneath it. Her shoulders were narrow, her frame as small as a child's. Her hips were pronounced but slender, her legs well shaped and unmistakably feminine. "I just wanted to make sure you're all right," he said lamely, knowing it was a poor excuse.

"I'm fine. Now if you would just close the door . . ."

James hesitated for only a moment. Then he reached inside, grabbed the pile of her clothes, and dutifully stepped out again, closing the door with a loud click.

"Hey, what are you doing with my clothes?"

"Having them fumigated, then cleaned."

There was a short pause. "And what am I supposed to do while they're being cleaned?"

"You stay here until dinner," James said calmly, ignoring her apprehensive tone. "Why do you think I doubled the breakfast order? We can't have you starving, which I'm sure you must be after the appetite you displayed last night."

He gathered her clothes together and was about to place them in a laundry bag when something occurred to him. Examining the labels, he saw that she was a size six. She would need something else to wear tonight if he wanted to take her to the Captain's Ball. And he did, James noted without much surprise. She had gotten under his skin, and he was starting to accept that more and more easily. He would let her stay in his cabin, and he would find out all her secrets before too long. She was vulnerable, he knew that much, and she was enchanting. The combination was delicious. He threw a light jacket over one shoulder and left the suite, whistling loudly.

A glorious sun was shining over the ocean, and Oliver and Zeebo hailed him as he angled around the deck.

"Well, well, you're looking chipper, James," Zeebo said in his nasal voice. "I trust you slept well?"

James laughed as if Zeebo had said something extremely funny, making Oliver grab his aching head.

"Not so loud, please," Oliver moaned. "I'm having trouble finding the deck."

"I sympathize with you, Oliver," James said, patting his back. "But I'm afraid you asked for it."

Zeebo wasn't amused. He looked at James with a

worried frown. "James, there's been another burglary," he reported bluntly, causing his friend to stop cold.

"Oh . . . really?"

Oliver filled him in. "The Steins."

James nodded. "The elderly couple who beat us at bridge the other night."

"Yes, they woke up a little while ago to discover that someone actually went through their belongings while they slept."

James was stunned. "If this keeps up, the thief should be able to open a boutique by the end of the trip."

"Just as long as it isn't an art gallery," Zeebo added nervously. "Then again, he'd have to be handy at opening three-inch-thick steel safes."

"Or have the combination," Oliver added, making Zeebo blanch.

James reassured him. "The purser is the only one with the combination, besides the captain. And of course you have yours in your safe deposit box." Zeebo nodded. "And you gave the numbers to me. Well, then, you're all right. The combination is hidden in my cabin, and I'm the only one who knows where it is." His mind darted at once to Susan, who was now all alone in the suite. She didn't know where the combination was. She didn't even know there *was* one. There was no reason to suspect anything, and yet the whole situation seemed very odd.

"What's the matter, James?" Zeebo asked. "You look worried."

He gave them a humorless grin. "Someone fleeced my wallet of two thousand dollars last night."

This news was met by looks of stunned surprise. "Oh, no, not you too. Why didn't you say anything?" Zeebo noticed the purser across the deck and hailed him over frantically. "My good man, there's been yet another theft," he announced.

The purser was a little man in a navy uniform with strands of hair pasted with perspiration across his scalp. "That's dreadful, sir. Would you please provide me the details?" Oliver filled him in with considerable drama. "The captain has doubled the guards at the safe," the purser informed them when he had heard the whole story. "We're doing the best we can to prevent any further incidents."

James's uncle Henry had sauntered up next to them, overhearing the last part of the man's speech. "Impressive," Henry said pleasantly, patting the nervous little man on the back. "Doubled the guards? I hope they do the same for the dining room." He looked around the group with a twinkle in his eye. "It seems someone has pilfered every table."

James silenced a groan at the thought of Susan darting around the dining room as if it were a gourmet wonderland. "Pinched the food?" Oliver repeated, incredulous. "Now that's going a bit far, isn't it?"

Uncle Henry smiled. "Even a couple of steaks."

James tried a laugh, which was met by stony silence. "Uh—that's terrible," he amended, trying to look sober and concerned.

The purser frowned. "It could be a stowaway."

James said nothing, but he watched the man carefully. He felt very protective of Susan; surely none of this could be attributed to her . . .

"Yes, sir, I've seen this sort of pattern before. A stowaway usually hides by day and scavenges by night. We've had evidence of that on this trip. Whoever it was even had the nerve to climb into the captain's cabin and take some of his best sherry. Must have been a mountain climber. Went over the side and right through the captain's bedroom window while he slept."

James almost choked.

"This gets more and more interesting," Oliver said. "This burglar is a stowaway, a pickpocket, and an expert climber with very good taste in sherry." This sounded so outlandish that he immediately burst out laughing.

Everyone laughed along with him except for the purser, who continued to frown thoughtfully. "It is possible, sir, but we can't say at this time. And now that Mr. Bentley's wallet was fleeced"—he paused and shook his head in sheer dismay—"I'm afraid we're not sure what we have on our hands."

"Well, I'm sure you'll take care of it," Oliver said rather loftily. "After all, you're the expert on this sort of thing, not us."

James's uncle tactfully changed the subject, letting the distressed purser slip away. "Looks like a wonderful day for iceberg watching, don't you think?"

"Yes," Oliver agreed. "I understand that we're following the exact same route as the *Titanic*."

"Not funny! Really, Oliver, you don't know when to stop," Zeebo shrieked, walking off in a huff as Oliver went after him, apparently contrite.

"Well, good morning, Uncle," James said cheerfully.

The older man examined him with interest. "You look

awfully happy today, James. A considerable difference from yesterday, I might add."

James laughed. He couldn't help it, he felt rejuvenated since he'd met Susan. "I'm just feeling better, that's all. If you'll excuse me, I have some shopping to do. I've never had much use for the stores on these ships, but today I've got to find something special for someone."

Uncle Henry's eyes lit up. "Aha! Well, since it isn't *my* birthday, I'll assume some lovely young lady has captured your attentions."

James's broad smile was a dead giveaway.

"Ah, so I was right," Henry noted. "Is it serious?"

James shrugged, enjoying his happiness. "It's too soon to know."

Uncle Henry became as solicitous and interested as a mother hen. "Oh, let me guess. Is it one of Lady Prudences's daughters?"

The very thought caused James to burst into laughter. "Not even warm, Uncle Henry."

Henry waited expectantly, but since no further clues were forthcoming, he backed off with deferential politeness. "Well, happy hunting, James. Enjoy yourself, my boy." He smiled a little. "Oh, to be young again." He strode off with a trace of a smile still on his face, leaving James to fend for himself.

If ever there was a time to believe in fairy godmothers, Susan expected that hers was around and already working miracles. She sat in the tub, too refreshed and relaxed to bring herself to leave. Every time the bath cooled, she turned the faucet on with her foot and let scalding water heat the tub back up again, while she reveled in the luxury.

"This more than makes up for two days in that gunnysack," she said to herself. "Melinka, you are one lucky stowaway."

Her mind drifted lazily to James, her unwitting host. He was being terribly accommodating. She didn't know why he was putting up with her like this, but she had long ago learned not to question her luck. He was allowing her to be here, and for now, that was all that mattered. She would cross her next bridge if, and when, she came to it.

Suddenly she heard the door to the suite open, and then the sound of someone moving around the living room. For several minutes she wasn't sure if it was Peters with her food or James with her clothes. She hoped it was James. Whoever it was, he was heading for the bedroom, and the bathroom door was still ajar. The last thing she needed was to be caught in a bathtub.

As she cringed behind the shower curtain, the bedroom door opened slowly. Susan contemplated ducking under the water and holding her breath, but dismissed the idea when she realized there would be no camouflage since the bubbles were long gone. The towel rack was just out of her reach, and she was afraid to stand up for fear of making too much noise.

The sounds continued, and she grew more and more alarmed. If it was James, why didn't he say something?

Her eyes darted around until they caught sight of the mirror. From her angle she could see a flash of someone passing back and forth. Surely it couldn't be James. He had no reason to act this stealthily. Reaching for the only likely weapon at hand, the long-handled back brush, she readied herself to clobber whoever might come in.

The footsteps went back and forth in the bedroom for a few more minutes until Susan thought she would scream from the suspense. Drawers opened and closed. The closet door was opened and there were sounds of shuffling and—searching? It sounded as if someone was . . . looking for something.

Whoever that someone was, he was now directly outside her door, his hand on the knob. The man hesitated, apparently undecided as to whether or not he wanted to enter the bathroom. Susan stared at the hand, praying with all her might that she wouldn't get to see its owner. It was a powerful-looking hand, unadorned except for a simple but unusual ring on its middle finger. The band was gold, and there was a crest of some sort that looked like a pair of hawks or eagles.

The door opened another inch, and Susan decided to take the bull by the horns. "James William Bentley!" she called out suddenly. "If you want to live long enough to see James William II, you had better not come in here!"

That did the trick. The culprit let go of the handle and the hand with the ring disappeared. A moment later she heard the bedroom door open and close, and then the door to the suite.

Susan wasted no time in scrambling out of the huge tub and wrapping herself in a burgundy bath towel. Dashing out of the bathroom, she stopped dead in her tracks as she surveyed the scene in the bedroom. The place was a shambles. Clothes had been pulled carelessly out of drawers and dumped onto the floor, books and magazines had been strewn around, and the closet had been ruthlessly cleaned out. Stunned, she tiptoed into the living room and saw that the same savage handiwork was evidenced there.

It was definitely time to leave.

Suddenly, the door to the suite opened and Susan began to back away, clutching the towel around her body. A cart loaded with food was pushed into the room. "Here you are, sir!" Peters called out. "Just as you ordered!"

CHAPTER
Five

JAMES SPENT ALL OF the next day and night looking for Susan. He searched every nook and cranny of the ship, skipping lunch, then dinner, in a fruitless pursuit. She had, quite simply, vanished. And so had all of his valuables, but not, thank goodness, the code to Zeebo's vault. The thief, whoever he was, must have seen the numbers but had not realized their worth.

But where was Susan? Had *she* seen the culprit? Was she hiding in fear for her life? Had the thief caught her as she tried to escape, and was he now holding her somewhere on board? Worst of all—could Susan herself somehow be to blame? Hating himself for even considering the possibility, he dismissed the idea as soon as it had come into his head.

It just wasn't possible. He had seen for himself that she took only what was necessary for survival—including the Winchesters' steaks. He laughed when he thought of that, but only for a moment. He was too concerned with what might have happened to Susan.

At dusk, James stood in the second-class passage in the stern, looking down at the canvas. It was now closed off. Someone had locked it up, but he didn't have a clue as to who had done it—or why. A chain had been placed around it, and a padlock secured the two ends of it.

"Where is she?" he muttered in frustration, his fist hitting thc railing. "Where could she possibly have gone?"

"I'm right behind you, silly. You just haven't been looking in the right places."

James whipped around and looked at the apparition standing in the moonlight. Dressed in his clothes, Susan looked adorable as she adjusted the left cuff, which had fallen down over her foot onto the floor. She pulled up the belt, closed the jacket again, and flexed her arms in an attempt to find her hands, which had disappeared inside the sleeves.

"Where have you been?" James demanded. "I've been going mad trying to find you. I was tempted to climb inside that contraption of yours again, but someone has locked it up, as you can see."

"I know," Susan moaned. "Along with my luggage. Now where am I supposed to stay? And what will I wear?"

James gave her a closer look, blinking when he recognized his own clothing hanging from her slender form. "Oh. I wondered where my best jacket had gone. I thought the thief took it."

Susan's face darkened with thoughts of that afternoon. Overwhelmed, she rushed into James's arms, surprising him immensely. She had hidden all day, and now she was throwing herself at him. She felt soft and tantalizing against his chest, and he struggled to comfort her without sweeping her into a much more sensual embrace. "He almost saw me naked in the bathtub," she burst out.

He stroked her wild cloud of hair. "Susan," James asked gently, "did you see him?"

"No!" she said vehemently. "No, I didn't." She hesitated a second and amended, "Well . . . I did, a little."

James gave her a quizzical look. "I don't get it—you did or you didn't see him."

"I saw his hand," she said.

He laughed. "Could you describe it in detail?"

Susan was not deterred. "He was wearing an unusual ring. I think there was a bird or something in the design and two other little etchings on it."

James stopped laughing, waiting for more information.

Susan shrugged. "That's it. I was too far away to get the details, but I think if I saw that ring again, I'd recognize it."

He frowned. "But you didn't see his face?"

"Oh, no. Not at all." She shivered. "All I knew was that I had to get out of your cabin as fast as possible. The food arrived a minute later. When Peters saw the mess, he called security immediately. I didn't want to get caught naked in your bathtub."

"Hmmm, I can see your point," James said. He held her away from him and laughed softly. "I like your outfit. I might not have guessed we have the exact same taste in clothes."

"Which reminds me," Susan said. "I'd like mine back."

He gave her a little smile. "If I return them, will you join me for dinner and a dance this evening?"

Not looking the least bit surprised, Susan frowned in dismay. "I have nothing to wear to a formal dinner and dance."

"A minor detail, and one I've already seen to." James gallantly held out his arm. "My lady, if you please."

Susan was hesitant. "I don't know . . . I've been to so much trouble to keep out of sight, and now you want me to make a grand appearance."

"Relax, Cinderella. No one will look twice when they see you, unless it's because of your beauty. You'll knock them dead."

"That's what I'm afraid of," she muttered, but she followed him willingly back to his cabin.

They passed a number of people on the way, and although many of them did seem to notice Susan's unusual getup, no one said anything after a quick glance at James.

Susan began to relax, and had almost forgotten all about her predicament once they were in the safety of James's cabin. The first things she saw were her own clothes hanging in the open closet. Next to them was a stunning creation made of red taffeta and tulle. Susan approached it slowly, lifted it by the hanger, and held it up to her body. She looked at James. "For *me?*"

"I had the tailor use your old clothes to determine the

size. He's very experienced at last-minute shipboard estimates, so it should be a good fit."

"It's beautiful," she said softly as she fingered the tiny, expertly hand-sewn stitches inside the bodice. "And expensive."

"Never mind that."

"But I do mind. I didn't expect anything like this."

"I know you didn't. That's what makes it fun." James smiled graciously, an easy smile that cut straight to her heart. This was obviously a man who was used to giving gifts and who enjoyed it. It wasn't the cost of the dress, or his ability to pay for it, that affected her. It was the aura of command, the assumption that he could benefit his world and everyone in it, including her. There was something extremely attractive about it, yet it made her vaguely uneasy at the same time. She wasn't used to owing anything to anyone; she didn't want to start now. Especially not to a man as charming and enticing as this one.

Susan shook her head stubbornly, reluctant to comply. "But what if I'm spotted? Wouldn't they arrest me and throw me in the brig for being a stowaway?"

"I've already payed your fare," James announced. He took the dress and tossed it onto the loveseat. "You know, you look lovely in men's trousers."

"Wait just a second!" She pushed away from him. "You paid my fare?"

"I got you a nice little cabin as well. About the same size as this waiting room. But a hundred times bigger than your previous accommodations." He dug into his pocket and handed her a set of keys.

Susan stared at them. "Second class," she observed blankly.

He gave her an exasperated look. "Do you want to move back to your—ah, tent?"

"That's not what I meant!" she stormed at him, her eyes blazing. "What right did you have to purchase a whole cabin for me? I'm not your responsibility! You haven't adopted me, nor I you!"

He looked genuinely surprised, but only for a moment. His tanned, winsome face betrayed no further emotion other than a little amusement, which enraged Susan even more. "This may come as a big shock to you, James Bentley Whatever, but I'm not interested in becoming your charity case. I am also less than interested in being your current plaything, or this month's little doll to dress up!"

He looked completely unruffled, crossing his arms patiently in front of him. "All I've done is to present you with a few small gifts. I have no ulterior motive, and I can assure you that my intentions are completely honorable."

Susan seethed with anger. "Don't be rididulous, James. I would hardly call a fancy designer dress and a whole cabin 'a few small gifts.'"

"But I enjoyed giving them to you. Why can't you accept them without making such a fuss?" His eyes flashed for a moment, and Susan felt a surge of triumph. So she had found a chink in the armor, at last, she thought, not even sure why she had felt the need to.

"Because they're excessive, that's why. They are inappropriate."

"Not to me," he said, uncrossing his arms and shifting his stance from one long leg to the other. "You needed a dress and you needed a cabin. It was quite simple."

Susan advanced on him, her hands on her hips. She had no idea that she made a rather comical picture, dressed in those hopelessly oversized clothes; she was too intent on getting her point across, no matter what. "I did not ask for these things. I did not want them."

"Ah, yes, but I'd be willing to bet you'll accept them."

"Don't be so sure!" she cried, her eyes narrowing. "It may seem amazing to you, your lordship, but I was perfectly happy with my stowaway status. Accommodations and all. Maybe they didn't seem very nice to you, but I rigged them up, they were my discovery, and I was a little proud of my ingenuity. I didn't ask for any help, and I wasn't hurting anyone."

"Well, your clever little hideaway has been locked up," he pointed out. "What would you have done for shelter tonight, may I ask?"

"That would have been my problem," she retorted with a toss of her head. "And that is the whole point. I have lived by my own wits for two years, and I haven't been beholden to anyone."

James broke his maddeningly nonchalant pose to stare at her with unbridled curiosity. "You've been running around like this for two years?"

"Yes," she answered with a lift of her chin. "I've been traveling around Europe, if you must know, getting jobs where I could, and sacking out in barns and woodsheds when I couldn't. I've met an incredible number of very nice people, many of whom helped me in many ways. But one thing I haven't *ever* been interested in is a sugar daddy."

The last two words appeared to hit him like a bomb. "You are an ungrateful and contrary woman, Susan!" he exploded, his hazel eyes boring into her with an anger that both frightened and exhilarated her. His wrath was obviously something to be reckoned with, but she felt a distinct thrill to know that she had at last cracked his infuriatingly cool facade.

"You seem oblivious to the fact that you have been breaking the law, and that I have been put in the position of abetting your crime." He sighed angrily and reached into a drawer, pulling out a piece of paper. "I wasn't going to tell you this until later, because I didn't want to ruin a perfectly pleasant evening, but—" He broke off and handed the paper to her.

Susan's eyes opened wide in shock. "It's a subpoena!" She scanned the document quickly and looked at him. "I'm accused of . . . theft of service." She looked up him, hurt and confused. "Why, you louse. You snitched on me!"

"I had no choice," he informed her coolly. "It was under my lawyer's advice. I wired him in New York to meet you at the pier when we dock. He'll represent you. It's just a formality. You'll appear for a hearing next month. You're a first offender, so you'll probably get a fine and a slap on the wrist."

"Or a jail sentence!"

He smiled. "Oh, no. I wouldn't let them do that to you. Then again, if that happens, I'll come and visit you the first Tuesday of every month." The smile broadened. "If you like, I'll bring you a cake with a file in it."

Susan groaned. "So how much do I owe you for all this? I'm going to pay you back, you know. I still don't intend to accept your charity."

James gave her a captivating smile that made it difficult for her to think. "Exactly two thousand dollars."

"Oh. I see. The amount of my reward for finding your watch," Susan said. "Maybe that's not the way I would have planned to spend the money, but at least we're even."

He shrugged. "Sort of." She eyed him warily, and he let out a helpless sigh. "The thief stole my watch."

Cinderella never had it this good, Susan thought as she finished the last of her Jamaican coffee and a sinfully delicious English trifle. She sat across from James in the large ballroom of the ship, the windows of which featured a complete three-hundred-and-sixty-degree view of the moonlit ocean. The twelve-piece orchestra was playing a Cole Porter tune, and Susan had happily forgotten all about her lofty values concerning living free.

The lights had been dimmed enough to highlight the view, and every so often a passing iceberg caught everyone's attention, causing a pleasant flurry of excitement to travel around the room.

Susan tore her eyes away from the latest mountain of ice to find that James was staring at her. Again.

"You've been staring at me all evening," she said nervously. "That last iceberg was well worth a glance, at least."

"The last time I passed up iceberg watching, I ended up finding you. Shouldn't I again?"

Susan smiled a little. "Is that a compliment?"

He hesitated, but then nodded. "Of course. I didn't mean to get you into trouble, you know. I really didn't have any choice."

"I know." She sighed. "And I didn't mean to drag you into my problems. Unfortunately, you kind of fell into them."

"I take it you're something of an adventurer," he said.

"I'm an international spy," she teased.

"Right, and I'm James Bond."

"So, Mr. Bond," she said, lowering her voice and adopting an exaggerated Russian accent. "At last we meet." And picking up a knife, she placed a napkin over it and aimed it at his face just as the waiter came over to refill their wineglasses. "Don't move, Mr. Bond, or I'll be forced to shoot."

Taken by surprise, the waiter spilled some wine on the tablecloth. He would surely have raised his hands in surrender, if James and Susan hadn't both burst into a fit of giggles.

Relieved, the waiter caught on. "Oh, jolly good joke, sir." He looked at Susan warily. "If you don't mind, miss?" He uncovered the knife and placed it back on the table. "Wouldn't want it to misfire, now, would we?"

When he was gone, Susan continued laughing, and James reached out suddenly and took her hand. "You are a kook," he announced with a look of definite approval.

"I know," she responded happily.

"Oh, yes. It's an image you have to keep up, right?"

She shrugged. "Maybe. But we all have our little facades, don't we? You certainly have yours." But she said it lightly, without malice, and he nodded.

"I suppose so." His hand remained curled around hers, and her heart began beating rapidly against her chest. The flimsy bodice of the dress seemed like the scantiest of coverings all of a sudden, as if her true feelings were about to be revealed no matter what she did. "You look incredible in that dress," he murmured, startling her. The way his eyes were focused on it, she could swear he was imagining what it would look like if it were off of her altogether.

"Thank you," she said, her voice fluttering along with her heart. "I've never worn anything quite like it before."

His hand tightened around hers and his thumb began to stroke her fingers with a slow, sensual rhythm. "Was it so wrong of me to give it to you? It wasn't generous of me at all, believe me. I did it for my own selfish reasons. I wanted to see if you would look outrageously sexy in it." He gave her a rakish little smile. "And you do."

Susan tried to hide the fact that she was trembling, but it was no good. "You—you must think I'm terribly inexperienced," she murmured, astonished at the power of her reaction to him.

"Oh, no," he said, his voice lowering to a husky whisper as his thumb continued its erotic journey over her hand. "Your experiences are of great interest to me. And I'm becoming more and more interested in adding to them."

"I'm not a child, you know."

"Oh, I know, I know." His eyes sparkled.

"But perhaps you're not enough of one." She wasn't sure why she said that, but it definitely got to him. The thumb stopped moving, and he sat back and looked at her. He thought it over for a moment and then nodded. "Yes, I suppose you are right about that. I guess I just grew up too fast."

"Or not at all," Susan mused. "Without the childhood, there can never really be an adult."

He frowned and cocked his head to one side. "Interesting theory. But not necessarily true." He laughed. "I really did have a rotten childhood, corny as it sounds."

Susan rolled her eyes. "Poor little rich boy?"

"Something like that." He got up and held out a hand. "Let's go outside. I can use some cool air on my face."

She took her coat over her shoulders and went with him into the moonlight. The moon was almost full now, and they strolled casually to the stern in comfortable silence. Occasionally they passed another couple, the men decked out in black tie and the women in brilliantly colored gowns. It was like being inside a fairy tale, one that she wasn't entirely comfortable with. There was something false about it. Not for them, obviously—but for her. She didn't really belong here, and she had the odd feeling that at midnight the clock would strike and she would have to run back to where she belonged.

"You're thinking about all these people, aren't you?" he asked quietly, reading her mind. "And you're thinking that you don't fit in."

She said nothing. Instead she took his hand. "Is

being rich as good as it looks?" she asked.

"Yes, it is. But that doesn't mean it isn't complicated."

"You mean you would have liked to postpone it until you could earn it for yourself?" Susan said it without thinking, and she was very surprised when James's hand in hers suddenly tensed up.

When they reached the stern, he let go of her and leaned against the rail. "This is our favorite spot, isn't it?" he asked. "Right over your former accommodations."

"You changed the subject." She came to him and made a circle on his chest with her finger. When he suddenly took her hand and looked at her, she caught her breath.

"Maybe I don't want to talk about it." He slipped his arms around her and let them play lightly against her back. "What I would like to know about is you. You've hardly told me anything at all."

She gave him one of her mischievous looks. "I know."

He nodded, pulling her in close with sudden force. "That was your plan, wasn't it? It adds to the mystery of the little stowaway without an identity. You're not going to tell me anything unless I pry it out of you." The wind ruffled his hair slightly, and he drew her even closer. "You may be a little surprised at my methods."

"You've already turned me in," she said breathlessly. "What else can you do?"

He answered by kissing her in a sudden rush that was devastating in its directness. His sense of command had returned in full force, but this time there was something inevitable about it, as if he couldn't have prevented this kiss any more than she could have. His mouth took hers in a flash of sensual rightness, moving slowly to prolong the delicious sensation. Susan stood stock-still for a moment, and then, without warning, her arms found their way around his neck and she was kissing him back with all the ardor that was in her.

He was strong and warm and she felt safe somehow with him, as if he wouldn't harm her no matter what. He was a safe harbor in the midst of her wanderings, and for the first time in two years, she felt she had found a place where she wanted to linger.

The kiss broke slowly, both of them tinged by the wonder of it. Then Susan managed a tiny laugh. "Well, you distracted me, all right." Her eyes twinkled as she gave him a sunny smile. "But I still want to know more about you."

He chuckled, but then his face grew stern. "All right. How does a few hundred million sound?"

Susan shrugged. "The same as one hundred million. What's the difference?"

"Well, there is a difference, believe me."

"My heart bleeds."

He turned away from her, staring out to sea. "My father abandoned me to the whims of my mother's family."

"And they brought you up with every ounce of privilege, as well as their fancy background and entrée into society. What's wrong with that?"

James gave a bitter laugh, and suddenly she knew that she had hit a very tender spot. His face changed, darkening as he turned toward her. "They despised me."

Susan stiffened. "I— That's hard to believe."

"Why? They had lost everything in the Depression except their titles," James explained. "They still had their blue blood—they just didn't have any money to go along with it. The family had to find a way to stay solvent until something came along." He looked at Susan for a second and turned back to the ocean. "What came along was my father."

"I see," Susan said quietly.

James chuckled, running a hand through his hair. "Would you believe it? My father was actually in love with my mother. He was head over heels for her." He waited for a moment and then said, "They were living in separate quarters a year after I was born."

"My God." Susan could think of nothing consoling to say. She put her hand on his arm, and after a moment he covered her hand with his own. "And so you became your mother's responsibility," she surmised.

"Yes, to the chagrin of her entire family. I was a constant reminder to them that they had acquired a huge sum of money in such a crass way. But like most people who have been poor for too long, they squandered most of it." He looked at Susan and delivered another punch. "In return for bailing them out, my father demanded a very high price, and that was my salvation."

Susan brightened. "But he wanted you. You didn't have to be an outsider any longer."

His hand closed around hers. "I was fifteen when I entered public school in Massachusetts. Talk about culture shock. I came home black and blue after my first day. But my father was determined to knock the pansy out of me. And he did. By the end of that first year, I could take any kid in that schoolyard."

Susan studied him. "You seem no worse for wear."

"Oh, but I am. I became incredibly jaded about everything." He looked at her with a sad little smile. "Haven't you noticed?"

She looked at him for a long time, thinking about it. "No," she said at last. "I think you *like* the idea of being jaded. It appeals to you. It's an image you've cultivated, one that suits you well. You get to play the part of the wounded, bored aristocrat who bails mischievous young women out of trouble because he has nothing better to do. But you're not fooling me, James Bentley."

"What do you mean?" he asked, bristling. "You can see I haven't had such a soft life after all."

"No one's life is easy," she scoffed. "You could have had it plenty worse. Stop complaining."

"I'm not. You asked me about myself, and I told you."

"But you adore the idea of the poor little rich boy, I can tell." She turned and looked at him squarely, her small, pointed face alive with challenge. "Give it up, James. It's boring."

He arched an eyebrow. "Are you saying I bore you?"

"No, but I think you're boring yourself. You've got a life to live. Go and live it."

"Now that is profound," he said dryly. "I'll have to remember that."

A small silence fell between them. "You're not going to tell me anything about yourself, are you?" he said after a while. "You'll keep changing the subject."

She gave him a sexy little smile. "You changed the

subject last time, if you recall. And quite effectively, too."

"Are you suggesting I change it again?"

She summoned her courage, stood up on her toes, and took his face in her hands. Leaning against him, she brushed his mouth gently with hers, tasting him with just a provocative glance. She repeated the gesture again and again, teasing him until at last he gripped her firmly and kissed her for real, slanting his mouth over hers and seeking her tongue with his own.

Susan was lost in a swirl of sensation, drinking in the magnetic appeal of this complex, wildly attractive man. She was thrilled that he desired her, but that thrill was overshadowed by her own driving need for him.

It was getting cold. He led her back to the dining room without a word, holding her tightly around the waist in silent possession. An iceberg passed nearby, a huge diamond floating on the ocean.

They sat back down at their table and James ordered cordials and more coffee. Susan closed her eyes for a moment, savoring the evening, and said to herself, "If only Sherry Schumaker could see me now."

James laughed. "Who?"

"Sherry Schumaker," Susan said as if anyone would know. "Miss Wonderful. The class know-it-all. Miss Prom Queen herself. The girl most likely."

James perked up. "Does this mean you're about to reveal some information?"

"Well, it's not all that mysterious. I come from a town in Idaho."

"Idaho?"

"You see?" she said with a pained expression. "I knew you'd react that way."

"Sorry. It's just that I've never known anyone from Idaho."

"No one has." She sighed. "It's like I'm from another planet. Especially to someone like you."

His eyes lit with understanding. "So that's it!"

"Well, I'm not exactly what you're used to, am I? Not after the life you've led."

"Now, that is not fair," he said, pausing as the waiter brought their cordials and then taking a sip. "I just wanted to know why you were stowing away on a ship."

She looked surprised. "Because I didn't have any money. Why else?"

"Well, I have to confess I didn't know. Somehow it seemed as if you were doing it because you wanted to."

"I did want to. I was enjoying it. But I still didn't have any money. A lack of funds isn't a tragedy, you know."

"No, I don't know, do I? I've never had the chance to find out. Do you mean you've just been bumming around like this for years?"

She gazed at him haughtily and took a sip of her drink. "I wouldn't describe it that way. I have simply been traveling on my own, experiencing different things, and leaving the future up to fortune."

He looked nonplussed. "But—what did you do before that?"

She shrugged. "I went to school. I had a job in a drugstore for a while. I went to college for two years, but I got very bored there." She looked away and then back at him. "I have a restless nature. I don't like to stay in one place very long. I didn't want to tell you that, because—well, I didn't think you'd believe me. I figured you had me pegged as a funny little kook who needed to be rescued." She pinned him with the force of her gaze. "And I'm not."

"Oh. So I'm to believe that you're simply an original free spirit?"

"Yes!"

"Bull," he said, throwing down his napkin and tossing back his head to finish his drink. "You are glamorizing a nomadic existence that is merely covering up a dull, unhappy life."

"It's not dull, or unhappy. It was. That's why I left Idaho."

"But why go roaming around the world like a gypsy?"

"Because I like it!" she shouted at him. "I told you you wouldn't believe me!"

He looked at her for a long time. "Well, what are you planning to do next, may I ask?"

"People always ask me that. I don't know. I'll see when we arrive in New York."

"Don't you ever make plans?" he insisted.

"When I feel like it."

His impatience grew as he shifted in his chair. "Well, do you feel like it now?"

She smiled brilliantly. "Why? Are you extending an invitation?"

He looked outraged all of a sudden, and he stood up abruptly. "You are impossible," he announced through clenched teeth. "Perhaps you would like to be escorted back to your cabin?" He held out his arm and Susan stood up, planning on taking his arm but certainly not on trotting away before the evening had ended.

She was about to lay her hand on his arm when she noticed his third finger. There was a telltale band of blank white skin where a ring had recently been. James had obviously taken it off after wearing it for a long time. But why? Her hand caught her throat, and she froze.

CHAPTER
Six

"ARE YOU ALL RIGHT?" he asked, his former anger immediately dissipated.

"Uh, yes," she said. "I was just thinking that maybe the thief was in this room at this very minute." She had turned very pale.

"That would make him a first-class passenger, now wouldn't it?"

Susan looked around the room at all the people, trying frantically to see their fingers. After all, she thought, maybe James had just decided not to wear his ring tonight. Yes, of course, that must be it. Susan began thinking rapidly. "Then again, there is no way for a thief to get up here to first class." She looked at James for confirmation. "You said that yourself."

"Yes, I did say that, but something changed my

mind." He gave her a direct, accusing look. "Or should I say, *someone* changed my mind?"

Susan pointed at herself. "Me? Are you serious?"

"Quite," James said. "I understand that someone pinched a good bottle of sherry from the captain's cabin the other night."

"I didn't know it was the captain's cabin," Susan said indignantly, now that the tables had somehow turned. "I was climbing up to the next level when I passed his window. It was wide open, and wouldn't you know it, there was a delicious-looking lemon meringue pie just sitting there—"

"Next to a bottle of very good sherry," James added.

"Well . . . yes."

"So you sat in his cabin wolfing down his dessert and drinking his best sherry?"

"And took a nap in the captain's bed," she finished rather guiltily as James's uncle approached them.

"Slept in the captain's bed?" he repeated, looking amused. "Did I hear that correctly?" The man's pale blue eyes swept admiringly over her petite form. Uncle Henry smiled and looked at James expectantly. "Being at sea too long has dulled your manners, my boy."

"Oh, excuse me, Uncle. This is Susan Melinka."

"Oh, yes, the little pixie you were telling me about who stowed away, and, I might add, slept in the captain's bed."

"But I assure you," Susan said nervously, "the captain wasn't there at the time."

This produced a chuckle from both men, and Susan joined in, feeling that perhaps she was going to get away with this after all. But her smile died as she saw a tall, bearded man approaching her. He was wearing a uniform, and he did not look amused. He was heading straight for her, and she shrank back involuntarily.

He came straight up to the group and announced without preamble, "Good evening. I'm Captain Gerard." He looked at Uncle Henry. "Sir, may I assume this is your nephew?"

"Why, yes, this is my nephew, James Bentley."

The captain looked at Susan, who took a step backward. "And may I further assume that this young lady is the one who was reported to me?"

Susan took a deep breath and held out her hand bravely. "I'm Susan Melinka, sir. I believe I'm the one you're looking for."

The captain took the proffered hand, but it was quite clear that he did so out of sheer politeness. He merely touched it, and then dropped his own hand to his side. "I assure you, I have not been amused by your antics, young lady."

"I'm sorry, sir," Susan said, crestfallen. "I didn't mean any harm."

"You are quite lucky that your benefactor here has paid your passage. Because if I had been so fortunate as to have been there at the time you took my best sherry, you would now be spending the rest of this voyage in a very small room near the number-two engine reserved for only our most exclusive clientele. And I would have the only key."

Susan squirmed, and James frowned at the man, but he continued undaunted. "And may I add that you'll be getting a bill for the Winchesters' dinner, as well as for your other samplings."

Susan looked at James desperately, and he stepped in gallantly. "Oh, by the way, Captain," he said, "I understand that a reward has been offered for the return of the jewelry that was taken."

"Yes," the captain said. "Ten thousand dollars." He looked meaningfully at Susan. "But why limit ourselves to just one thief?"

Susan turned white. "Are you implying—"

James jumped in again. "Let's not forget the fact that Susan saw. . ." He hesitated at his next words. ". . . *one* of the thieves."

The captain looked confused. "What are you people talking about?"

Susan explained in a rush. "Look, I can understand why you'd think that I'm responsible for all of the thefts on board, but honestly, all I did was stow away and take enough food to hold body and soul together. I don't know a thing about the rest of it, except—"

"Except for what?" The captain was clearly on the edge of his patience. She began again, stuttering in her attempt to get it all straight, and once again, James came to her rescue. He explained about Susan and how he had found her, and how he had left her taking a bath in his suite.

The captain listened to the story with several quick nods of his head, and then snorted. "So while your cabin was being burglarized," he summed up, "Ms. Melinka here was conveniently taking a bath. Then she conveniently disappears, and finally ends up sitting here in first-class passage having a wonderful old time." He looked at James and then at Susan, and added one final note. "And all is to be forgiven."

"Precisely," James said sternly. "And as long as she is with me, she has an alibi."

"Is that so?" The captain waved for someone to join them, and James looked surprised when that someone turned out to be Zeebo. His face was very somber, and he approached them with a worried, distraught air. Oliver traipsed along with him, obviously under the influence again.

"They're gone!" Zeebo cried as soon as he drew near enough for them to hear. "My paintings! Stolen right out of my safety deposit box in broad daylight."

The captain gave the group a hard look. "Someone had to have had the combination. There wasn't a scratch on the lock."

James looked wildly at Susan, who stared back at him in complete innocence. "Well, don't look at me!" she cried, backing away. "Where would I get the combination from?"

Oliver was the first to answer. "From James's drawer, this morning." He pointed a drunken finger at her. "After you robbed him, of course."

James spoke up calmly. "But I still have Zeebo's combination." He held it up, dangling it convincingly. "It never left my pocket."

Zeebo frowned and took out his copy, comparing it to the one James was holding. They did not match at all. "She switched them on you," Zeebo announced morosely.

"She probably had her accomplice go to the vault," Zeebo mused miserably.

"Accomplice!" Susan cried. "What are you talking about? I don't have an accomplice!"

James ignored her along with everyone else. "So all we need is the list of people who were in the vault this afternoon, and we can narrow down who the thief must be."

"Well, I wasn't in the vault this afternoon," Susan said. She turned to James. "I was hiding in your uncle's cabin all day, if you must know."

Everyone looked at Henry. He was astonished. "Hiding in *my* cabin? How convenient." He looked at the captain. "That explains it. Out of her own mouth."

Susan felt trapped. "What did I say? What did I do?"

The captain gave a heavy sigh. "Henry's cabin was burglarized this afternoon."

Henry shook his head. "She didn't steal much. I went down to the vault this afternoon and placed everything of value inside a safety deposit box, which seemed like a wise move after all the thefts. But my room was in a shambles when I returned." He looked at Susan. "You didn't by any chance catch sight of the thief with the strange ring while you were hiding in my closet, did you?"

James said nothing, but he was frowning oddly, as if trying to figure something out.

Susan wanted to answer, but she couldn't speak. A terrible sense of dread had overcome her, and it intensified when the captain waved two security guards over.

"I'm sorry to have to do this," he said, "but I'm afraid I must. I have an obligation to the other passengers, and this has gone on long enough."

Susan reached for James's hand, and he took it, giving it a little squeeze. "Help," she whispered in a pitiful squeak.

Susan quickly decided that sleeping in a raft attached to the hull of the ship was better than her little prison bunk. Her new accommodation was all cold steel, with a protruding bed consisting of a mat and a pillow. The bathroom facilities were less than civilized, and the hum of the engine was enough to keep her up all night. The only thing was the ocean view afforded by the porthole. Unfortunately, if she was caught with the porthole open when the ship crested a good wave, her little room was splashed with sea water.

"I hate it in here!" she yelled, trying to make her voice heard above the drone of the engines. "I want breakfast."

She took her metal coffee cup and dragged it across the little iron bars of her door window. The noisemaker was just as futile as her voice. Finally she sat down on her bunk and began inventing ways to murder James William Bentley. Pushing him into the ocean would be handy, but he could probably swim. Clubbing him over the head was simple, but messy. Possibly she could lock him in a closet and starve him to death.

With a heavy sigh, she surveyed her situation once again. It was definitely bad. Very bad. She was dressed in her own clothes again, the red dress hanging on a hook on the wall. It swung back and forth in a desultory motion that only reminded her of how hopeless her predicament was.

Suddenly a familiar voice broke through the monotony. "Hello, in there!" James called to her cheerfully through the metal door. "I hope you slept well."

"You fink!" she said, and threw her cup at the small window on the door for emphasis.

James ducked, but then his face reappeared. "You can't possibly be mad at *me*."

"Who should I be angry at? You're the one who reported me. And you didn't do anything to convince the captain that I'm innocent of any further crimes. He thinks I'm a thief! Everyone does!"

"You are a thief," he said calmly. "Not an art thief, maybe, not a first-class burglar, but you have pilfered from time to time on board this ship. If anything, you're a nuisance, like a mosquito that won't go away."

"How flattering. I ought to—"

"You ought not," he interrupted her. "Remember, I'm on your side."

"Well, you have a strange way of showing it."

"Have I? What about last night?"

Susan shifted uncomfortably. That was what really hurt. There had been a special magic last night, a burgeoning rapport between them that had been shattered after the captain had ruined the evening. "It was nice, wasn't it?" she said bitterly. "But over."

"I rather enjoyed it myself," James said as he peered through the bars to get a better look at her. His voice was husky and persuasive. "If it wasn't for a few million dollars' worth of paintings being pinched, we'd probably have gone back to my cabin after a few more dances, partaken of an excellent bottle of champagne I was keeping chilled for the occasion, and then made passionate love."

Susan gave him the tough, street urchin look she had learned long ago. "You're pretty sure of yourself, aren't you?"

"So are you." He leaned against the door. "I see they were able to deliver your clothes. You'll be needing them if you want to look your best this morning."

Susan immediately brightened. "They're letting me go?"

"Uh—no, not quite."

Susan fell back. "Then why should I want to look my best?"

James cleared his throat. "It seems that you and I will be having breakfast together this morning."

Susan heard the sound of a key entering a lock. The door swung open, creaking on its hinges, but it wasn't her door.

The purser's hand appeared behind James, resting on his shoulder. "Sorry, sir. If you'll please be so good as to step inside."

James waved to her. "I'll be right next door," he announced.

Susan ran to the door and tried to peer out, but it was too late. She couldn't see anything except for the purser's hand gesturing as James went past him. A door opened and closed with an ominous bang, and before she could ask any questions, the purser was opening her own door and handing her a tray of food.

"If you'll be needing anything else, miss, don't hesitate to ask," he said politely.

She could only think of a few hundred things, none of which she was likely to get, so she took the tray and sat down. This was all very confusing. "James!" she called out. "Are you there?"

"I'm having my breakfast," he answered casually. "Would you care to join me? That is, in spirit."

"Where *are* you?"

His voice was maddeningly cheerful. "I'm right next door. We're in jail together. Thought I'd keep you company. Why do you ask?"

Susan was flabbergasted. "But . . . why you? I mean, you're a millionaire, after all. Why would a millionaire steal?"

"Oh, it happens all the time. Rich art connoisseurs who lust after unattainable masterpieces. Usually they find out about a stolen painting and put out a bid through the black market. Zeebo's paintings don't happen to be for sale, however, which makes them all the more desirable."

"And you took them?" she asked in a tiny little voice. After all, she *had* suspected him.

"No, of course not. I didn't say I did. I was merely explaining why a rich person would steal them."

"But you didn't."

"No."

"Then who did?"

"I really have no idea. But unfortunately, new evidence has pointed to me, and here I am."

Susan was completely baffled. She hated having to communicate like this. She wished she could see him. With all the confusion, he was still the only friend she had on this ship, and last night she had dared to think that he was becoming more than a friend. "What new evidence?" she asked, dreading the answer.

"Rather damning evidence, I'm afraid. It seems that most of the stolen goods have ended up in my cabin, although I have no idea how they got there. Most of them except the paintings, that is."

"Very suspicious," Susan said. "So where did you hide the paintings?"

James said nothing, and Susan took a large bite of toast, hugely enjoying the fact that he was in the same boat as she.

"How does it feel?" she asked, taking a sip of orange juice.

"What?" he returned murderously.

"To be accused of being a thief."

"I resent your accusations. I am no thief. If anything, you are. After all, you are a bona fide stowaway. And I did catch you red-handed in the act of taking food."

"Circumstantial, my dear Mr. Watson."

"Not really," James answered. "I do have eyes, you know."

"So, guilty with an explanation."

"Spare me."

She waited a moment, finishing her toast, and decided that she needed companionship more than anything else. "Hey!" she called out.

"Hey, yourself."

"Stick your head out the port window and I'll do the same."

James laughed. "Now why would I want to do that?"

"So we can see each other."

There was a moment of hesitation.

"Go on," Susan called after him. She could hear him opening the window, and she ran to her own window, carefully easing her head through it. There was James, peering at her from his own tiny opening, looking decidedly cross.

"Hi," she said sheepishly.

He grunted a response.

"Look, we've got to work together," she urged. "We're both stuck here, you know."

"I noticed," he said, his face still murderously grim.

Susan thought quickly. Obviously someone had planted all those stolen goods in his cabin in order to link him to her as an accomplice. She considered all the possible suspects, including all the people who had been robbed. Any one of them could have robbed themselves in order to throw off suspicion.

"Look, I'm sorry," Susan called out to him. "I know you're not the art thief, James."

"Oh, really? How do you know that?"

"I just know."

"Woman's intuition?" he asked dryly.

"No. I'm just putting all the pieces together, that's all."

"Thinking again? Please don't. It taxes my credulity."

Susan refused to buckle under his sarcasm. The ship rolled slightly, and they both hung on, tasting a splash of salt water as it sprayed against the ship. "What about your friend Oliver?" she persisted. "Could he be the culprit?"

"He's not my friend," James said. "I believe he's Zeebo's cousin or some such relation."

"Maybe Zeebo stole the paintings from himself in

order to get the insurance money. He then has the money and still retains the paintings."

James laughed. "You should open up a detective agency."

"This is serious, James!"

He laughed again. "It's certainly cured the doldrums around here, I can tell you that. Before I met you, I was happily enjoying a quiet little identity crisis when you came along and spoiled it."

"Why would you have an identity crisis?" Susan asked seriously.

"Why not?" he answered impatiently. "I'm allowed."

"You were probably just complaining," she said with a sigh. "You've been complaining since I met you."

"I have not!"

"But you have everything a person could want. Don't tell me you're still stuck on that business about your background. Really, James."

"This is hardly the time to talk about that!" he snapped. "Right now we have to get out of here."

"Well, do you have any brilliant suggestions?"

He shrank back. "No. That is, not yet."

"Why don't you knock the purser out with your tray?"

"What?"

"You don't know karate, do you?"

"I am not James Bond, and I'm not going to accost the purser."

"You have to. We can sneak into Oliver's cabin. I'm sure the paintings are there."

"Why not the captain's cabin?" James asked with growing irritation. "Even if you don't find the paintings, you can help yourself to more of his sherry."

"Well, it was very good sherry."

James let out a yelp of sheer frustration, and ducked his head back inside. "You are impossible, woman!" he shouted.

"You're not helping any," she returned. She realized there was something about the situation that amused her. She could say anything she wanted and he had to listen. He wasn't used to being in a fix like this, and he had no idea how to handle it. "That's the trouble with you people," she sang out.

"What people?"

"You know," she said coyly. "You classy types. You're all know-it-alls."

"I've never heard it put quite that way."

"Well, it's time you did more listening."

"Do I have a choice?"

Susan fell back on her bunk and began to review the situation once again. She could hear him pacing back and forth, almost like a parody of what a prisoner was supposed to do.

Three hours later they hadn't had their lunch, nor had they had any other conversation. Susan continued to go over all the suspects, and James continued his pacing. Despite the noise from the engine, she could hear every move he made, and it was beginning to get on her nerves.

"Would you mind having a seat?" she asked him.

"Pacing helps me to think."

"Well, think more quietly," she said. "This is driving me crazy."

"Join the club," he said, and deliberately clumped back and forth.

She put her hands over her ears and sighed. All this bickering was getting them nowhere. "I think a truce is in order here."

"I'd settle for a cease-fire," James answered back. "My feet are killing me on this steel floor."

"This pillow isn't doing my ears any good either."

"A truce," he called out. "And let's shake on it. Come to your door." Susan looked up and saw his hand waving wildly, reaching out from between the bars of his door. She ran to her door and stretched out her hand as far as it would go, reaching until her fingertips met his.

The touch of his hand sent a little shiver through her, and he did nothing to end the contact. "Your hand is lovely," he said quietly. "If we're still here tonight, can I make love to your hand?"

Susan couldn't help giggling, and she snatched her hand back inside. "What kind of girl do you think I am?"

At that moment the purser appeared. There were two burly sailors with him. They opened both doors.

Susan stepped outside quickly, glad to be free of the tiny room, and she smiled when she saw James doing the same thing. She had a sudden urge to rush into his arms, but the purser was addressing them.

"The captain would like you both to join him for lunch in his cabin," he announced primly.

James and Susan exchanged surprised looks, which changed rapidly into broad smiles. But the smiles faded just as quickly when the two sailors produced a set of handcuffs.

"Are those necessary?" she asked with a stab of dismay.

"I'm sorry, miss," the purser said. "Captain's orders." She took a deep breath and held out her hands, but they attached only one handcuff to her left wrist. She started with surprise when the other one was attached to James's right wrist.

James looked at her quizzically, raised their bound wrists, and examined the brace. "Does this mean that I don't have to wait until tonight?"

CHAPTER
Seven

THE CAPTAIN'S CABIN WAS all too familiar to Susan. When they entered, her eyes strayed automatically to the cabinet where she knew the sherry was stored. It now had a padlock on it.

The purser left them alone with the captain, who went to his cabinet, took out a key, and opened the padlock.

"Would either of you care for some very fine sherry?" He looked at Susan when he said that.

"I'd love some," Susan said nervously. She didn't know if he meant it or not.

"We'd be delighted," James added with an air of distinct authority. He gave Susan a warning glance. "I won't beat around the bush," he said as he accepted a glass of sherry. "I believe Susan is quite innocent."

"If you say so, then so do I," the captain agreed.

Susan stared at them both in amazement.

The captain handed her a glass of sherry. "You're quite lucky to have such an ally in Mr. Bentley, young lady. It was his idea to be locked in a cell next to yours."

"You mean—you set me up?"

James looked down for a moment, but then his eyes met hers. "He had to know the truth," he explained. "I volunteered to become a prison mate in the hope that you would tell me whatever was on your mind."

"Exactly," Captain Gerard said. "All evidence pointed to you, you see. I had every right to leave you in the brig until we reached New York. And I still do," he added emphatically. He gestured with his glass at James. "You'll be in Mr. Bentley's charge for the rest of this voyage."

"That is still not fair," Susan said, bristling. "I'm not a child who needs to be watched every minute. I haven't been convicted of any crime."

"Think of him as your parole officer," the captain said, ignoring her protest. "And you don't leave his side until this trip is over." He gave her a rueful smile. "It's certainly better than being stuck in the brig the whole time."

She looked at James. He had a huge grin on his face, as if he was greatly looking forward to the prospect of being in charge of her. He lifted up their connected hands and waved them back and forth for emphasis, but Susan yanked her hand down, pulling his along with it. "I'd prefer the brig," she announced stubbornly.

"No, you wouldn't," the captain said, dismissing her. "Now don't be foolish. Besides, I'm the captain of this ship, and I'm issuing a direct order."

"Yes, sir." She saluted. "Will there be anything else?"

The captain put down his glass, and it made a decisive clink on the table. "Yes. You are confined to your cabin in second class unless accompanied by Mr. Bentley. Your cabin will be locked from the outside and only your parole officer and I will have the key."

"And whose idea was that?" Susan asked hotly as she looked at James.

"Mine," the captain said. "And I might remind you that you are to be delivered to the authorities when we reach New York."

Susan stared down at her lap. She felt like bursting into tears, but that was out of the question. She didn't want to be made to look any more foolish than she already felt. There was nothing to do but maintain what remained of her dignity as best she could. She lifted her chin and faced Captain Gerard with all the poise she could muster. "Is there anything else?" she asked with such quiet pride that both men looked at her in unexpected admiration.

"Yes, there is," the captain said. "Please understand that the thefts occurring on this voyage are extremely serious, and you are still under suspicion. All I have are my own instincts and Mr. Bentley's word that you are innocent."

Susan thought for a moment, and she couldn't help interrupting. "But why do I have to be penalized like this? The thief could be anyone at all—even James." She added that rather brazenly, and the captain flinched.

"True," he said, "but that's not the point. I have to trust someone, and he is the most likely candidate. If you are kept under confinement and the thefts continue, you will be cleared."

"If the thefts stop, that won't prove anything."

"I realize that, young lady," the captain said. "But as I said, I've got to make some rules here, and my decisions will be obeyed or I'll have your head. We are in a very perilous situation here. Not only is this ship being picked clean by a very clever thief, but there have been an unusual number of iceberg spottings for this latitude. It's not only unusual, but extremely dangerous. I've put in a double watch every night since we left Southampton, and the crew is exhausted." He gave Susan a final, pointed look. "So I don't need any more monkey business from you. Am I understood, Ms. Melinka?"

Susan nodded. "I understand."

They all looked at each other for a long moment. Then there was a sharp knock on the door. The captain opened it to one of his officers. "More icebergs, sir. A lot of them. Got the whole radar screen looking like a mine field, sir."

The captain turned to his guests. "I really did want you to join me for lunch, but it looks as though I may be gone for a few hours. However, please feel free to stay and enjoy the meal. It will be served in a few minutes."

He left with his officer, and Susan fell back in her chair with considerable relief. "Well, at least I'm out of jail." She tried to reach for her glass, and realized that she was still handcuffed to James. "Oh, no!" they groaned in unison.

There was a knock on the door. "Come in!" James called out.

The purser wheeled in a lunch cart. "Lunch, miss. Captain's compliments."

Susan held up the handcuffs. "We have a slight problem here. Can you get the captain to unlock these? He left in kind of a hurry."

"Sorry, miss. He's very busy for the next few hours. We've had orders not to disturb him." He walked over to the large window, which was partially shaded from the late afternoon sun, and lifted the shade dramatically.

"Oh, my God," Susan cried, and ran over to look, dragging James along. The ocean was a veritable forest of icebergs, each one glinting like a huge diamond in the sun. The ship was steering slowly between them, pursuing an endless obstacle course. Susan stared in awe at an iceberg that passed right outside the window. It was an immense, jagged mountain of ice, with thousands of clustered protrusions. The sun's reflection off the gleaming surface was so strong that she had to shield her eyes.

"Have you ever seen anything like that in your life?" she asked breathlessly.

"None of us ever have, miss," the purser explained. "It's a beautiful sight, but also very dangerous. One of these beauties is what sank the *Titanic,* you know."

"Let's not talk about that," James said. "Now I understand why we are behind schedule."

"Quite, sir." The purser stood with them a moment longer and then left them alone, promising to alert the captain as soon as possible about the handcuffs.

James turned to Susan as she stared at the eerie sight on the ocean. "Amazing, isn't it? We'll get a different view from the ballroom tonight."

"Ballroom?" Susan looked at him. He smiled at her. "But aren't I confined to quarters?"

He jiggled the handcuffs. "You are confined to me. And where I go, you will go."

That was an understatement. As they attempted to eat lunch, they discovered that one-handed dining was a very perilous venture.

"Pass me the salt, will you?" Susan asked, trying to balance a forkful of peas while James was tugging at her other hand as he cut his meat.

"Certainly." He reached across the table and got the salt shaker, which caused an inadvertent tug on the handcuffs. The motion jostled Susan, and the peas spilled all over her plate. She ended up picking them individually and popping them into her mouth.

"I wonder what there is for dessert," she said.

"Let's get up and look." They rose together and inched toward the cart, where James lifted a silver lid to reveal a raspberry torte. "We'll have to cut this," he said. "Can you reach that knife?"

By the time they finished, Susan was exhausted. "If every meal were like this, I wouldn't bother half the time," she said, falling back in her chair and dragging James with her.

"It could be a new diet," James said cheerfully. "The Handcuff Diet. You do it with a partner, and you lose weight together."

Susan laughed along with him. "Oh, dear," she said. "I think we're getting slaphappy."

"Well, it's no wonder. We were cooped up in jail cells all day, and now we're handcuffed together." It sounded extremely funny all of a sudden, and they both burst into raucous laughter. Every time the laughter started to die down, one of them would start again, and they kept on laughing for five whole minutes.

"I could ravish you right here," James said conversationally, producing another fit of giggles from her. "But it might be difficult."

"Let's go over to the window and watch the icebergs again," she suggested. They got up in unison and walked over to the window, which was now filled with the slanting rays of twilight. The icebergs still stretched into the horizon, as far as they could see, and they stood for a long moment absorbing the strange beauty of the sight.

"Thanks for getting me out of the brig," she said at last.

"It was my pleasure."

She turned toward him. "I can't believe that. You were stuck down there all day along with me."

"I enjoyed the company."

"But we were bickering most of the time!" She chuckled. "Of course you knew all along. You're a wonderful actor."

He bowed. "Thank you, thank you. I'd like to thank my producer, my director . . . and you, for providing the inspiration."

"Me?"

"Of course. I wanted you out of there. After all, you weren't much use to me locked up out of sight."

She gave him a coy little glance. "And of what use am I out here?"

He turned her toward him and held her with his free arm. Before she could say anything, his mouth descended on hers and he was kissing her deeply, privately, with all the pent-up passion that had been brewing between them all day long. Susan felt herself ignite almost at once, and she grew heady with the overpowering sensations he aroused in her. She wanted him suddenly, fiercely, wanted to shake free of all inhibitions and abandon herself to him. The depth of her reaction stunned her, but she didn't care. He had the power to do this to her, and she knew instinctively that it was rare and beautiful. And what was more, she knew without question that the same magic was conquering him.

They kissed and kissed again, their bound hands straining against the lock. James's free hand began a restless, hungry quest over her body, molding her tiny waist, drawing dizzy lines across her bottom, and brushing lightly across her small breasts in a move that caused her to moan with delight.

"James," she whispered, leaning against him, "do you think the captain will be back soon?"

"God, I hope not," he murmured back, kissing a fiery trail down her neck.

"But the handcuffs . . ." She managed a very frustrated little laugh.

"Stranger things have been done," he said. He stopped and held her shoulders, looking down at her with sensual gravity. A careless shock of hair had fallen over his forehead, and his eyes glinted with determination as he looked into her face. "I want to make love to you, Susan. I have ever since I first saw you."

"But not like this, James. Not here. Not now."

They faced each other wordlessly, and then there was a sharp rap on the door. The purser entered, looked at them, and announced, "My assistant will have the key down here in about an hour. I'm sorry I can't get it sooner, but the captain cannot be disturbed."

James caught Susan's eye with a knowing look that made her heart jump. "Later," he whispered, giving her hand a little squeeze. "And then we'll have all the time in the world."

"I'll pick you up at eight tonight," James said as he prepared to lock Susan in her cabin. He felt horribly strange doing that, but they had promised the captain, and she didn't seem to mind. "The icebergs are supposed to be spectacular tonight. The purser said there would be hundreds of them floating around out there. A regular obstacle course, he said. Plus the weather promises to be clear, and warmer than usual." Susan smiled but said nothing. "I'm sorry to have to do this," he said wretchedly.

She didn't answer.

"Susan, please. This will all be over soon."

She looked alarmed when he said that, and he tried again. "I'm sure everything will come out all right."

Her eyes slanted back and forth, and still she said nothing. He thought back to that first night he had met her, when she had been so reluctant to talk, and realized that she retreated into silence whenever she was worried or unsure about something. Determined to conquer her anxiety, he took her in his arms.

"I promise, Susan. I'll get the best lawyers in New York if I have to." He grinned. "And don't worry, they all owe me favors." She looked up at him with her huge blue eyes and he stifled a groan. All he really wanted to do was make love to her, but this was hardly the moment. Not when he had to lock her inside. So he did the next best thing. "I'll see you in a while," he whispered, drawing her close and kissing her gently. Her lips were very sweet, and the kiss lasted longer than he expected.

She gave him an odd, pointed look, slipped out of his arms, and closed the door. After a moment's hesitation, he decided to leave her alone for a while and he walked back to the deck.

He tried to distract himself thinking about his business in New York and Boston. He had nothing but the usual grind to look forward to when he got back. It would be one management meeting after another. Eighteen departments, three stock portfolios to read over for approval, the hated budget report, and the projections for the next quarter all loomed ahead. This trip was supposed to clear his head for all that, and instead it made him want to run away from it all.

Perhaps Susan would want to extend her vacation in New York before heading home. She'd be a welcome relief at night from all those headaches. He could put her up at a hotel if she wanted, or they could risk write-ups in the gossip columns if she stayed at his apartment. The thought of spending a whole uninterrupted weekend with Susan Melinka made his blood jump.

He realized soberly that she had affected him much more than he had originally wanted. She had been intriguing at first, amusing, but not someone to make a formal commitment to. Now, he realized with a profound shock, he was actually falling for her. The little nymph who had been a delicious challenge at first was now bewitching him, but for some reason he found it perfectly delightful. He threw back his head as he stood at the ship's rail and laughed into the open air.

"Glad to find you so merry, my boy." It was his uncle, strolling along the deck in an outrageously British-looking getup of sailing whites and a blue-and-white ascot. "I've been looking all over for you," he added.

James laughed. "For you to come down to second class means that you were looking *all* over for me."

His uncle made a face. "Really, James. That's an exaggeration."

James arched an eyebrow. "Oh, come now, Uncle. Surely all those years without any money must have made you at least a bit understanding of others. In a way I always respected you for holding your own. You hung on until my father came along."

"Thank you, James," Henry said, patting him on the back. "Too bad we can't say the same for the Winchesters."

"What on earth do you mean?"

"Bankrupt," Henry said. "They haven't got a penny."

James saw where his uncle was leading. "That doesn't make them art thieves."

"I quite agree," Henry averred. "But rumor has it that Dun and Bradstreet wired the captain early this morning. Seems they are wanted back in London for some routine questioning regarding some missing holdings."

James started to speak, but his uncle stopped him. "This is purely confidential information. I haven't had time to confirm any of this, so for heaven's sake, James, don't go blabbering it to anyone until the captain brings it up."

"Word of honor," James promised.

Henry nodded and changed the subject. "Terrible mess this young lady has gotten you into."

"Not really." James couldn't help smiling at the

thought of Susan. She was a handful, all right, but she had been exactly what he needed.

His uncle gave him a warning look. "Be careful. The newspapers would just love to get wind of this."

"Don't worry," James said. "If it looks as though that might happen, I'll end this affair at once."

Henry nodded his approval. "A little shipboard dalliance, eh, James? Oh, if I were only younger." He chuckled and walked away, leaving James to himself.

James stared out to sea, wondering what he had gotten himself into. Whatever it was, it was too late to back out. He was already in for the duration.

As she showered in the tiny bathroom, Susan's mind kept returning to James. He had been a convenient helper at first, not the only person over the last two years who had come to her aid in an awkward situation. But he had refused to let her go. Something about him had kept her coming back to him again and again, and she knew the reasons went way beyond her current predicament.

She hadn't dreamed that he could have any real problems or that he would need someone to confide in. But James *had* confided in her, and the knowledge that he trusted her with such personal information was thrilling. She felt privileged somehow, and responsible for the secrets he had told her.

He was a fascinating mix of English breeding and American ambition. Apparently he found the combination unsettling, but to her it was endlessly intriguing. Susan realized with a flash of insight that it wasn't so much what had been bothering him, but that he had seen fit to share it with her that touched her so.

Happy, she began to sing loudly in the shower, stopping only to rinse the shampoo out of her hair.

"Don't stop!" James called from the outer room. "Sing another chorus!"

Susan stepped out of the shower, mortified. "You could have knocked," she said.

His voice was very near, and with a sinking heart, she realized that she had left the only bath towel lying on the bed.

"Would you mind stepping out onto the deck while I get dressed?"

"Sorry," James said. "But I have my orders."

"Orders? What orders?"

"The captain gave me strict orders not to let you out of my sight," James explained.

"Very funny. Please, James, let me get dressed in peace."

She listened to his footsteps as he approached the door and turned the handle. But the door didn't open. "Oh, no," he said, and tried the door again.

"Oh, no, what?" Susan asked.

James snickered. "Apparently I left the door locked from the outside." He tried it a few more times, still with no luck.

"Use your key."

"I can't do that," James answered. "There's no keyhole on the inside. And it's obvious from the marks on the inside doorlock that the captain purposely had the lock removed so that you couldn't let yourself out. I'm afraid we're trapped in here."

"Oh, no!" Susan stood just inside the bathroom door, totally naked and trembling with cold. "Uh—would you mind handing me that towel?" she asked, feeling utterly foolish.

"What—this towel?" Susan saw him dangling the towel, and knew he was teasing her.

"Oh, come on, James. Just toss it over here, will you?"

He held it in front of him, just out of her reach. She made a murderous sound, and he tossed it over in her direction, turning his back as he did.

"You're a complete gentleman," she complimented him, relieved.

"Mother would have it no other way."

Grateful, Susan wrapped herself in the towel and stepped out of the bathroom to discover James perched on the bed. Next to him was a large box.

"What's this?" she asked.

"Open it."

Inside was an ice blue dress interwoven with gold thread that practically floated out of the box. It was an airy confection that seemed to be held together by a series of tiny straps. Susan lifted it and held it up. It looked like something a Greek goddess would wear. "It's beautiful, James," she said softly. "Thank you."

"Well, at least you're learning how to accept a gift without biting my head off," he said.

"I'm certainly acquiring quite a wardrobe on this voyage," she said. "Are you trying out for the part of my fairy godmother?"

"Hardly," James said. "I just didn't want you to be seen in the same dress two days in a row."

Susan laughed uproariously. "Heaven forbid," she crowed. "What would the Vanderbilts say? Why, Robin Leach would have nothing to do with us ever again."

"Are you making fun of me?"

"Yes."

James gave an exaggerated sigh. "I knew you couldn't accept it gracefully. Well, back to business as usual."

"Oh, James. I do like it, really. And I thanked you sincerely. Can't you understand how much I've valued my independence?"

James nodded. "Independence comes easily to you," he said slowly. "I had to fight for mine."

"Oh, rubbish. Everyone fights for his own independence," she said. "It's a part of life."

Startled, James was speechless as she grabbed the dress and retreated to the bathroom. "Be right out," she promised.

She emerged twenty minutes later, and enjoyed the enormous satisfaction of seeing James sit upright as if he had been struck by a thunderbolt. The dress floated around her, accentuating the subtle curves of her slight figure. She felt light, almost weightless in it, as if she had acquired a new identity.

"I'm ready," she said softly.

He turned to look at her, his expression reverent and wondering at the same time. "God, you look exquisite," he breathed, his voice barely above a whisper. Susan thanked him quietly, filled with the essence of being a woman.

"I *feel* beautiful," she confessed, the layers of the dress fluttering around her.

"No," he said. "You can never be beautiful. It's not your style. I've been with enough merely beautiful women to recognize something special."

"Is special better than beautiful?"

"It's more than better. It's different."

Susan bit her lip. "How so?"

He stood up and came to her, resting his hands on her bare arms. His words were hypnotic as he began a light, erotic stroking. "You do not look like anyone or anything I have ever seen. You don't look glamorous, or fashionable, or even elegant. You're above all that." He kissed her forehead and then her mouth. "You look like a goddess."

Susan swayed slightly, then leaned against him for support. Her breasts crushed softly against the starched white of his shirtfront, and she realized that she was trembling.

James looked deep into her eyes, capturing them with an intimacy that went straight to her heart. "What are you doing to me?" she whispered.

A glimmer of mischief stole into his eyes. "I'm guarding you, my dear. I'm watching you very, very closely."

"I—I think I like this arrangement," she admitted.

Mesmerized, James bent to capture her lips with his, their mouths meeting in a burst of flame that threatened to overpower them. *Now,* Susan thought. *It's going to happen now.* Her heart thudded wildly against him, and she closed her eyes, abandoning herself to a force she had no wish to conquer.

CHAPTER
Eight

SUSAN GAVE IN TO the tiny, arousing kisses James placed across her face and down her bare throat, letting her head fall back. Her breath was coming in short, uneven gasps, and she heard his voice through a haze of passion.

"You are delicious," James murmured. "I don't think I will ever be able to get enough of you, but I'm damned well going to try."

"James," was all Susan could say as she gently sat on the bed, too weak with passion to stand. James sat down beside her, pulling him in her arms.

His hands claimed every inch of her, drawing dizzy, arousing lines, and Susan was lost in a world of utter sensation. His strong, elegant hands spoke to her, telling her of his admiration and desire. They moved daringly over her breasts and slid beneath the layers of her dress to lovingly seek the softness of her thighs.

Suddenly he stood up, staring down at her, his eyes revealing the tide of emotions coursing through him. He tugged at the black studs of his dress shirt, revealing a strong, taut chest dusted lightly with hair as it fell away. Susan looked up at him in awe, all self-consciousness gone, replaced by a longing too powerful to deny. She sat up to help him remove the rest of his clothes, letting them fall in a random pile next to the bed.

When at last he stood before her, Susan couldn't move. He was strong and lean and powerful, and for a moment she felt shy again. But this was James—her friend, her protector. And she loved him. Susan reached out to him. "Come here," she said with a soft, encouraging smile.

James knelt down to her on the bed, swinging one long leg over her and slipping the other leg between her thighs. "So soft," he murmured, and kissed the tip of her nose.

Closing her eyes, Susan caught her breath as she felt her body respond to the feel of him.

Gently, James touched her shoulders, drawing the narrow straps of the dress downward. She lifted her arms to help him as he slid the dress over her small, firm breasts. He stopped when they were bared to him, admiring her beauty. With one finger he began to tease the pale pink tip of one breast, while his hand cupped the other one, savoring its softness. He lowered his mouth to a taut nipple, suckling it with a slow, maddening rhythm, and Susan felt light-headed with pleasure.

When the remaining folds of the flimsy material between them proved too confining, James slid the dress down her body, revealing her surprisingly full hips and slender legs. She was wearing only the scantiest pair of white lacy briefs, and he slid those down her legs with a deep sigh of longing. When she was fully bared to him at last, James sat back and gazed at her body, his eyes full of admiration at the sight of her.

Susan had never felt more vulnerable, and yet she felt sure, too. She knew James wanted her as much as she wanted him; she could see it in his eyes. Reaching out one small hand, she traced long circles on his flat stomach, teasing him, until finally her hand dipped lower. James closed his eyes and groaned, as she began a slow, rhythmic stroking that drove him wild. Thrilled that she could please him, Susan pressed closer, saying with her body what her heart was feeling.

"You bewitch me," James said huskily. He put his strong arms around her small frame and crushed her to him, kissing her with a deep, yearning intimacy. They leaned back together on the bed as they kissed, James's hands roaming over her body, finding the wells of deepest response.

Shifting slightly, Susan offered a silent invitation, and James read her movements instantly. Positioning himself above her, he nudged her thighs apart with one knee and joined them with a fluid grace that caused a gasp of pure pleasure to escape from her throat.

They found their rhythms slowly, moving carefully at first, and then with increased ardor. Their souls met, tearing down every last barrier between them. Susan wrapped her legs around him, opening herself to him completely, and James slid his arms beneath her to hold her to him as closely as possible. Susan felt herself spinning out of control as she welcomed his body to hers. She was spilling over the edge, murmuring little phrases of passion, bringing James to heaven along with her. Time suspended for one long, glorious moment, and then they were still.

After holding each other in silence, both too overwhelmed for words, Susan finally opened her eyes with the greatest reluctance. She smiled when she saw James's face, completely relaxed and sated; she knew without question that she looked exactly the same way. James turned to her and they smiled at each other, gazing into each other's eyes. Snuggling closer, they both drifted off to sleep, the smiles still on their faces.

It was much later when they heard someone outside the door, jolting them awake. "Quick!" Susan urged. "See who it is, James! We're locked in here, don't forget."

James leaped up and ran to the door, as Susan pulled the covers around her.

"Hello out there! We're locked in here! *Help!*" Susan couldn't help giggling. It all seemed so silly. And she realized, she wasn't really sure she wanted rescuing, after all.

"Who's in there?" a faint, wary voice answered. It sounded like a young boy.

"Listen, can you get the purser?" James called eagerly through the door. "We're locked in here."

"Well . . ." The voice sounded skeptical.

"I'll give you ten dollars," James offered.

There was a pause. "Can I have the money first?"

James reached for his wallet and fished out a ten-dollar bill. He was about to slip it under the door, when Susan ran to him and stopped him. Tearing the money neatly in half, she slipped only one half under the door.

"What's this?" the voice asked, bewildered.

"You get the other half when we get out of here."

James looked at her. "Very clever," he said. "Where did you learn that?"

She shrugged, pleased that he was impressed at her resourcefulness. "I've learned a thing or two in my travels. I wasn't born yesterday, you know."

James burst out laughing. "I think you got it from some old movie."

She smiled up at him, the look of a woman with a secret on her face. Their eyes met, and held, and Susan realized at that precise moment that she had fallen—head over heels—in love with James William Bentley. Her heart seemed to open up and embrace him from across the room, and suddenly nothing else mattered in all the world.

They were very late for dinner, but no one seemed to mind. The string orchestra was playing baroque music, the lights had been dimmed, and several couples were making the most of the dance floor. Dinner was served continuously throughout the evening, so there was no need to arrive at any specific time.

Susan was hoping for a small, private corner table, where they could watch the icebergs and engage in quiet, intimate conversation. But the maître d' approached them as soon as they entered the room, addressing them with polite formality.

"The captain requests your presence at his table, sir."

"The captain?" Susan swallowed hard, wondering why the captain had made such a request. Perhaps he wanted to keep close tabs on her himself. The thought was infuriating. She tossed back her head and marched after the maître d', determined to charm the captain.

They followed the maître d' to the long table in the center of the dining area, and Susan was surprised to see that she already knew half the people there. Besides the captain were Uncle Henry, Zeebo, and an elderly couple that looked very familiar.

"The Winchesters," James supplied helpfully. "You remember them—you took their steaks."

Susan gulped and asked about the other couple.

"The Steins. The thief cleaned them out yesterday."

Susan swallowed nervously, and recognized the last person at the table. "Oh, and there's Oliver," she said brightly, "the thief."

"Susan!" James warned under his breath.

"Look for the ring," Susan whispered back as they neared the table.

The captain stood up, as did all the men. He gestured toward the two available seats, which were right next to his. To Susan's dismay, she was seated on the captain's right, with James on her left. Oliver was all the way at the other end, and would have to lean forward if she wanted to see him. Next to Oliver were James's uncle and Zeebo, and the two older couples sat across from each other in the middle. Taking a deep breath, Susan gave everyone her best smile.

The conversation quickly turned into a Ping Pong game played by too many people at once, and she could barely keep up. By the time she got through the fruit cup and cold fish dumplings, Susan was positive she would not attend a formal dinner party again as long as she lived. The diners never seemed to tire of the same three subjects—the thefts, money, and more such dinner parties on the London and New York social circuits. But the thefts by far dominated the conversation and Susan wanted to scream by the time she finished her soup. Every point was covered—what was taken, when, where, how much each item cost, and as Mrs. Winchester put it, "how dreadfully ghastly this whole affair was."

Zeebo was the most upset. He moaned that his Monets would surely end up in some hidden collection that would take decades to uncover. "It's a loss to the entire world," he kept repeating as Susan regarded him with sympathy. He never once complained about the money he had lost, only the paintings. But she knew they had to be somewhere on this ship, and there had to be a way to find them.

As the main course was served, she attempted to lighten the mood. "My goodness," she said, "I feel as if I'm in an Agatha Christie movie. All we need now is a Colonel Mustard with a full beard and a"— her words faltered as she realized that she was about to describe the captain—"hat," she ended meekly.

The captain didn't smile. He looked unmercifully tense but still in absolute command. James was smiling wickedly, and Susan felt utterly frayed. She was about to conclude that James was going to be no help at all, but then she felt his hand reaching for hers under the table. He found it, gave it a reassuring little squeeze, and took a long, hearty sip of wine.

Oliver suddenly spoke up to cut through the tension. "I propose a toast," he said cheerfully, and attempted to stand up, only to fall back in his seat. After another unsuccessful try he offered the toast. "To the thief."

Everyone reacted.

"Yes," Zeebo said without humor, looking around the table. "Whoever you are."

No one laughed, and the mock toast suddenly fell flat. Oliver's gaffe was excused as drunken humor.

"To romance," James suddenly broke in. He lifted his glass gaily as everyone turned toward him relieved. "To romance on the high seas."

"More like romantic intrigue," Uncle Henry said dryly.

The Steins were not amused. They had said little during the meal. In fact, when Susan had reached across earlier to hand him the cream, Mr. Stein had given her an unmistakably hostile look. Susan had returned it with her most lilting smile, which only caused Mrs. Stein to peer at her suspiciously.

But Oliver didn't quit. He finally managed to stand up, holding on to the edge of the table for support. "To wine, women, and icebergs," he said gaily. As he held his glass aloft, Susan's eyes widened, and her hand clutched James's convulsively under the table. There on Oliver's wrist was James's stolen watch.

James noticed it, but when Susan tried to say something, he gave her a quick shake of the head. "We'll need something more positive," he whispered to her.

"What could be more positive than that?" she asked, startled by his coolness.

He stood up suddenly and went over to Oliver.

"Come on, old boy, I think you've had enough."

Zeebo rose also and, taking the cue from James, helped Oliver to his feet. Oliver bowed graciously to the guests and then allowed Zeebo and James to escort him to his cabin. The Winchesters and the Steins got up to dance, and Susan watched them leave with a sinking sensation. Suddenly there was a tap on her hand. The captain was looking at her with interest. "So," he said with jocular gruffness, "it's just you and me, kid."

"How could you do that to me?" Susan wailed at James as they walked along the moonlit deck two hours later. "I thought I would die of boredom!"

James gave her a cheeky smile. "Why do I have the strangest feeling that you're angry with me?"

"How could you leave me alone for two whole hours with that man? He had me telling him my entire life story."

"I thought he might," James said, nodding. "It was a good idea. Now he knows you a little better, and he likes you."

"He does?"

"Of course. Didn't you behave yourself?"

"You better believe I did. After all, I didn't have much choice, did I? It was my golden opportunity to let him know what a decent, hardworking all-American girl I really am."

He grinned. "You see?"

Susan sighed. "It wasn't so bad, I guess. It's just that we were alone for all that time. Where did you go?"

"Just doing a little private investigating on my own." He frowned thoughtfully. "You didn't by chance happen to get a clear look at that ring on the thief the other day, did you?"

"I'm not sure," she said slowly. "It all happened so quickly. Why?"

"Oliver is not our man." James led her over to the railing, and looked around to be sure they were alone. "We've recovered almost all the stolen goods. Everything, that is, except the paintings—much to Zeebo's chagrin."

Susan beamed. "Where were they?"

"Hidden in Oliver's cabin," he said. "Hidden so well, I might add, that not even Oliver knew they were there." He held up his wrist to show her that he had his watch back. "In his drunken state, Oliver accidentally put my watch on instead of his own. It was hidden among his own personal articles."

Susan opened her mouth to protest, but James closed it with his hand. "No," he said. "Oliver is not the thief. He's just a poor dupe."

"Then who *is* the thief, James?"

He kissed her suddenly, then gave her a challenging look. "The man with the ring."

"But why not Oliver?"

"Because, my sweet, Oliver is rich. He was at the auction with Zeebo and could easily have outbid anyone including Zeebo for those paintings. In short, Oliver can have whatever he wants without stealing it."

"Maybe he's a kleptomaniac," Susan suggested, only to have James laugh.

"He may drink a little too much at times, but Oliver's all right. Really, Susan."

He tried to draw her close, but his laughter had made

her feel a little silly and she shied away. Five huge, lonely icebergs were floating out on the water, and Susan stared at them.

"Come on," James said. "I'll take you back to your cabin."

"By myself?" Susan asked bluntly, turning to face him.

"I promised the captain I'd have you back by midnight."

"But—" She caught herself short. She wasn't going to plead with him.

"Look, Susan, it's for the best tonight, all right? Trust me."

She searched his face, finding no answers. She struggled to hide her disappointment, but couldn't. "Tonight meant nothing to you?" she whispered.

James melted. "Of course it did. I've never been happier in my life."

"Then why are you changing on me like this? As if you don't trust me all of a sudden?"

"Oh, Susan, I trust you. It's just . . . well, I'm not sure about much right now." He sighed. "Look, I promised the captain I'd have you back in your cabin by midnight or you'll turn into a pumpkin," he said, trying to make her smile. James took her arm and began to walk.

Susan walked beside him quietly, hurt and anger welling up inside her. She had no idea why he wouldn't trust her. It was true that, at this point, no one was trusting anyone else on board this ship. But shouldn't it have been different with them?

She wanted to rush into his arms, to tell him that she

had somehow fallen in love with him, that she didn't care about anyone or anything but him. But she couldn't get herself to mouth the words. Her heart sank as he led her to her cabin, opened the door, and waited for her to go in.

"Good night, James," she whispered, her eyes clear but her face etched with unbearable sadness.

"Good night, little pixie," he said softly, looking into her eyes with a tender, if unreadable, expression.

He closed the door with a little click, locking her inside.

It was for her own good, James told her early the next morning, when he said it would be best for her to lie low and stay in the cabin for the day. She was a star witness, and he didn't want anything to happen to her. Now, as she lay in her bed watching the sun climb in the sky, she wished she had wired Idaho for money to get home—something she had doggedly avoided doing for two years. Better that her father bail her out than be humiliated like this.

James seemed to be changing before her eyes. Susan absolutely refused to give in to the grief she knew would consume her if she let it, so she concentrated on self-righteous anger instead. How dare he do this to her? How *dare* he? Had she been nothing more than a plaything for him, a shipboard amusement? He obviously suspected her, that much was clear. What would happen when they reached New York? Something had to be wrong. She simply couldn't believe that James would make love to her the way he had if he didn't love—and trust—her. It didn't make sense. Susan paced the small cabin impatiently, waiting for a chance to find out. *Something* was definitely up.

She jumped when there was a knock on the door in the middle of the morning, but decided to play it cool. No sense in salivating over the man.

"Go away," she called.

"I will not," James said firmly. "I'm coming in."

"What if I'm not dressed," she responded.

As he opened the door, Susan saw that James had a navy blue sports jacket thrown over his shoulder, and that he looked oddly self-contained. "I thought you said you weren't dressed."

"I thought you were a gentleman."

He tossed his navy jacket on the bed next to her and sat down. "That was before I succumbed to your charms."

His suave composure was in full force again, but there was something different about him. She turned away, but he grabbed for her, looking into her face.

"Now listen, you little vixen, because I'm not going to say this twice."

Her eyes were shooting sparks. "How persuasive of you. No woman could resist such charm."

Her answer only seemed to fuel his anger. "You lied to me. Why?"

"What?"

"That ring you saw on the thief. You lied when you said you only got a glimpse of it. It's not too far from the bath to the door. Close enough to make out a design on a ring. You got better than a glimpse, didn't you?"

Suddenly she was shaking. "Why should I lie about a thing like that?"

"To protect someone."

She was caught. "That's ridiculous. Who would I want to protect? I don't know anyone on this ship. Sometimes I don't even know myself."

"That's not the feeling I get. I think I know who the thief is, and if I'm right, then you lied to me about that ring." He took her in his arms and made her face him. "Now tell me, who were you trying to protect? And why?"

She was trapped. She thought quickly, frantically, but there was no way out of this. "I'm waiting," James said.

She winced at the anger and hurt in his tone. Overwhelmed, Susan made a mad dash for the door, but her flight was countered by a flying tackle from James.

"Let me go," she shouted as he brought her back to the bed.

"Who are you protecting?" he insisted, his voice murderous.

"Maybe myself," she said, wholly irritated.

James shook his head. "No way. I don't believe I've been harboring a criminal all this time."

"And why not?" she asked petulantly.

"Because I know," James said. "You're a small, harmless thief, not a felon. Just a general nuisance."

"A nuisance!" Now she was truly angry. She tried to push him away, but he didn't budge.

"Who are you protecting? And why?" His hands gripped her shoulders, and she stared.

There was a ring on his finger, where there had been

no ring before. But it was not the ring she had seen on the thief.

"What is it?" he asked.

"That ring," she said. "Do you always wear it?"

He seemed to cool a little. "Why?" he asked. He was looking at her very oddly. "Answer me."

"No, you answer me. Do you always wear it?"

"Most of the time," he shrugged. "Except after it was stolen the day you saw the . . ." His voice trailed off, his face relaxing with comprehension. "The day you saw the thief's ring," he said heavily.

CHAPTER
Nine

"YOU THOUGHT *I* WAS the thief?"

Susan said nothing.

"So, you were protecting *me?*" He said each word slowly, his voice rising.

Susan was a little out of breath. She looked up at him, and he let go of her. "Yes, and you certainly didn't deserve it after the way you finked on me."

"You were protecting me," he repeated, not even listening to her. He gave a funny little laugh and kissed her on the nose. "That's very sweet." He laughed again, this time more shrewdly. "It's also, my dear, a bit ridiculous."

"And why is it ridiculous? I see a ring on a thief, and suddenly you stop wearing yours." She gave him a challenging look. "I'd say it's a logical deduction. You simply want to add three Picassos to your private collection hidden in a vault somewhere in one of your mansions."

At that suggestion, James fell back on the bed, laughing hysterically.

Susan waited patiently. Obviously she had said something very funny. "Ha, ha," she said stonily. "What, may I ask, is so amusing?"

"Do you remember that art auction Zeebo attended?"

Susan nodded and then realized what was coming next. "You were there also?"

"As were Oliver, the Steins, the Winchesters, and, I might add, the Waleses."

Susan stopped. *"Who?"* She looked wildly at James. "You never mentioned them before. Are they on this ship, too?"

James howled with laughter. "I was talking about Prince Charles and Princess Diana."

"Oh," she said, still not quite sure what to think. "So, what does this all have to do with you?"

"Like our friend Oliver, I too could have easily outbid Zeebo—by a lot."

"But you didn't."

"No. Because I wasn't interested. But how was anyone to know that?" He sighed. "The point is that you weren't the only one who suspected me."

She was surprised. "No?"

He sat up and grinned ruefully. "The captain wasn't so sure about me either." He held up his finger and took off the ring. "One look at this white space on my finger, and the captain had my room searched. Without my permission, I might add."

She looked at him questioningly.

"No, he did not find the paintings."

"I didn't say anything," she said at once.

"But you were about to."

She sighed. "This is all very confusing."

James shook his head. "Not really. Only if you happen to be interested in it, which I am not—outside of clearing my name, and yours. There are far more interesting things on this ship." His eyes lit up mischievously, and he slid his arms around her, pulling her close.

Susan wriggled away. "Is that all you can do at a time like this?" she asked. "Shouldn't we be trying to find the thief and the paintings?"

James shrugged. "I already know the identity of the art thief, if that's what's bothering you."

Susan lit up. "Zeebo!" she concluded. "He wanted the insurance money."

James shook his head. "It's not Zeebo."

"The Winchesters," she said, pointing a finger at James. "That old coot was droning on all night about Picasso until my ears nearly fell off."

James smiled. "I thought so too, especially after I had some rather disturbing news about them. They are in the midst of bankruptcy proceedings back in London."

"How interesting," Susan said dryly. "Did you see the way his wife thumbed her nose at me all evening during dinner?"

James was looking away, his face suddenly drawn, and she touched his arm. All at once Susan knew who he was thinking about, and the knowledge stunned her.

"By the look on your face," she said softly, "I have a feeling there's only one suspect left."

"I've been betrayed," James said. "And by someone I've loved all my life." He was looking down at the floor, and Susan put her arms around him from behind.

"That ring," James asked her. "Could you describe the design on it?"

She took a breath. "Two birds and a shield of some kind. I really was too far away to make out details."

James shook his head. "You did just fine. Did the design look like this?" He picked up his jacket and placed it back on the bed, this time with the pocket showing. There was a design on it, a crest of a falcon facing an eagle with an arrow in its talons. To one side of the face was the sun shining brightly with rays. On the other was a half-moon.

Susan gasped. "Is that your family crest?"

"Uncle must have gone broke, and didn't tell anyone. He was always so proud."

"But not too proud to steal?" Susan added.

"Too proud not to. I'm afraid he's gone a bit off the deep end," James said. "Either way, there is no proof that he is the culprit."

"But there is," Susan said. "Me. I'm a star witness. I saw that ring."

James shook his head. "A thief who can steal my ring could also steal my uncle's. All he has to do is put it on his own finger, let a witness like yourself see it, and make you think my uncle is the thief."

Susan was impressed. "You should be his lawyer," she said. "That's certainly possible. Maybe he isn't the thief after all."

"He is," James said adamantly. "He told me so this morning when I cornered him. It's sad, Susan. He's quite a desperate man."

She gaped at him. "Well, then, it's all over, isn't it?" She shook her head several times. "It's a sad ending, but at least it's an ending." She patted his hand. "It'll be all right, James."

"I'm not so sure." James looked at her somberly. "If I try to turn him in, he'll destroy the paintings. And without the evidence"—he shrugged—"well, let's just say that with a good lawyer he could easily go free on this one. As much as this pains me, we have to do the right things. Uncle needs help." He looked at her as he said this, his heart in his eyes. Susan wanted desperately to help him, but she didn't have any idea what to do.

"Mission impossible," she said.

"Exactly." James sighed. "Hopeless."

"Unless we make him believe that we've recovered the paintings." She thought for a moment. "Then he wouldn't have a chance."

"That's ridiculous. He'll see that we haven't."

Susan disagreed. "He doesn't have to see that we don't; he only has to hear that we do."

James laughed, but only for a moment. His face grew serious as he considered her idea. "I guess it's possible," he said. "If he thinks we've recovered the goods, he might try to see if it's true."

"And I'll follow him," Susan said.

James stopped her. "You'll do no such thing."

"It has to be me," Susan argued. "You could never fit through the porthole. You're too big."

"What porthole?"

"In your bedroom. We certainly can't chase after him. He might spot us. This way I climb out the window, head to second-class deck, where he probably hid the paintings, and watch him check to see if they're still there."

James was frowning and shaking his head. "I don't like the sound of this at all. Sounds dangerous."

"Don't worry. The worst that could happen is that he wouldn't be fooled by us at all."

James gave her a very dark look. "No, that is not the worst that could happen. Not by a long shot."

All that evening James rehearsed his lines over and over with Susan. She kept reassuring him that everything would be fine, but something still didn't seem right to James. If his uncle was cornered, would he try something desperate? James looked at Susan, who was busily going over the last of the plan for the eighteenth time that night. The thought of any harm coming to her filled him with dread.

"I don't like it," he said again. "I say we call this off, and tell the authorities."

She looked at him. "That would bring a terrible scandal to your family, and you know you don't want that. We can wrap this up quietly, right here on the ship, without any fuss."

"Without any fuss? What do you call this? And what do you know about scandal?"

"Just what I read in the papers, which is the whole point."

James grimaced. "Don't think I don't know that. Uncle Henry has already used that as a threat."

"So it's settled. We must recover the paintings and sweep this whole thing under the proverbial rug."

James looked at her with deep appreciation. She was genuinely trying to help him. "You're a real friend in need, Susan," he said, kissing her hand. "But I'm worried about you. You could be hurt."

Susan laughed. "Oh, don't be foolish. He's not going to hurt *me*." Her face fell. "Oh, James! You think he might try to hurt you?"

James threw his tip sheet on the bed. "Oh, Susan, it's as if I don't know him anymore. Let's just tell the captain and call this whole thing off."

"No," Susan said stubbornly. "This is for the best, James. You know it is. Try to stay calm."

"I will." He studied her for a moment. "Are you sure you aren't doing this just for the adventure?"

She looked at him thoughtfully. "Well, I suppose that's part of it. That's what life is all about. But I want to help your uncle, too. And you, James. You can handle it. Trust me."

"Maybe a stroll on deck would help clear our heads," he suggested.

"My head is perfectly clear," Susan said, snuggling up to him. "If you need distraction, I can think of something much more entertaining than a stroll on the deck." Her hands slipped under his jersey and found bare skin. "Mmmm," she murmured. "Nice."

"Maybe you're right," he said with a lazy smile, closing his eyes. She pulled the shirt over his head and stroked his taut, bronze chest. He sat up and reached for her, removing her clothes and caressing each part of her body as it was revealed to him. First the slender shoulders; then the pert, soft breasts; then the sloping belly and tiny waist; and finally the slim, shapely legs.

She lay back and watched as he slid out of his jeans with an animal grace that aroused her as much as his touch. He lay down next to her, claiming her with strong hands that both coaxed and tormented her. She was astonished at the depths of her arousal. It was as if a small torch were heating her body, igniting every part of her. She twisted sensuously beneath him, and he gave a ragged sigh.

"Beautiful," he whispered. "So soft." His mouth descended gently onto her breast, drawing on it steadily with just the slightest pressure until she moaned. "Sweet Susan," he breathed, kissing her breast all around before moving to the other one to repeat the erotic stroke.

His hand slipped between her silky thighs while she was still on fire, finding her most sensitive spot and urging it into flames. The pleasure rippled through every part of her, until she needed him, needed more, needed everything he could give her.

"Please, James," she whispered heatedly. "Now."

He met her willingly, his powerful body uniting with hers. They fit together so well that she let out a sigh of pure ecstasy. Then their movements were long and slow, prolonging the pleasure even as they detained its release.

Her heart swelled as she clung to him. Love overwhelmed her, and yet she fought it. The worst thing in the world would be to surrender body and soul to him. He already had her body, and she knew he had her heart. But that last precious bit of self was hers to keep. She could give it up only at her own peril.

The pressure within her increased until she was helpless in its grasp. James's arms tightened convulsively around her, and together they shared the beauty of sheer passion.

Silence fell upon them and yet neither had stopped trembling. Susan had never experienced such joy, such a heightened rapport with anyone in her life. They had traveled to a special place together, a place only they could create.

James voiced her thoughts as he lifted his head and looked down at her. "You're mine, little angel," he stated simply. "You belong to me. I'll never let anyone else have you."

His words thrilled her, and yet she felt a protest rising in her throat. "No," she said in a strangled voice. She shook her head, willing her heart to stop its wild pounding. "No one can own me, James. Not even you."

He smiled a little and stroked her hair. "That's not what I said, Susan," he whispered gently. "You belong to me, but I can't own you. There's a difference, don't you know?"

Susan waited in the dark under the stairway next to James's cabin, thinking not about the scene they were about to play out, but about what he had said to her. She absorbed his words with a sense of shock. What had started out as a romantic lark had become much more serious than she had imagined. She had fallen in love with this man, and while she couldn't bear to think of her life without him, she couldn't realistically imagine what it would be like with him. They were so very different. She didn't even know how to get through a formal dinner party without dying of boredom, although if she did say so herself, she had done a nice job of faking it.

Filled with doubts, she shook her head. The one thing she had learned to prize was her independence. Despite some occasionally loony methods, she had done an admirable job of sustaining herself on two continents for two years. Life with James would mean giving up the chance to establish herself on her own, to complete the journey she had begun on her own. She didn't want her highly personal odyssey to come to such a conventional conclusion. She thought of her hometown paper, the *Method Star,* with a gossipy little item: *Hometown Girl Returns on Millionaire's Arm,* and groaned.

But she had to focus on the matter at hand. They knew that James's uncle took a stroll around the entire deck every evening before dinner. It was now dusk, and she had been waiting for twenty minutes. He should arrive any minute.

Ordering herself to shape up and stop all this useless fretting, she picked up the three sturdy tubes that were used to hold paintings. She had gotten them from Zeebo, who had explained that the three Picassos had been sealed in an identical manner.

She waited another ten minutes, growing tense, and more alert. A number of people had passed, but none of them was the right one. Susan peeked out from under the stairwell one more time, and froze. Henry was approaching from behind.

She jogged rapidly in place to make herself sound out of breath, and ducked out from under the stairwell so that she would be seen. Trying to look as if she was hiding a tremendous secret, she pounded on James's door.

"James," she called furtively. "James, let me in. Hurry. I have wonderful news."

James opened the door on cue, letting the light from his room spill onto her. She held up the tubes for all the world to see. "Look what I found," she said excitedly. "Zeebo will be so happy."

James lit up, looking surprised. "Oh, my goodness," he exclaimed, and Susan tried to glare at him without giving herself away. He was the worst actor she had ever seen. He took the tubes from her and drew her inside, but kept his voice loud enough for anyone outside to hear. "The stolen paintings! My God! Are you sure? Where did you find them?"

It was Susan's turn to deliver the final line. She was aware that her acting ability wasn't much better than his, but they had counted on the surprise element to disguise their lack of talent. Uncle Henry would hear only the key words, and, it was hoped, would do what they wanted. Waving her arms dramatically just inside the doorway, Susan proclaimed, "You'll never guess. Not in a million years."

He closed the door behind her, took her into his arms, and kissed her soundly. "We were terrible," he whispered fondly.

"Shhh," Susan warned. "I think he's outside the door."

He nodded, and with his arm around her waist, talked right into the crack in the door. "I never would have thought of hiding them there," he said.

"Your uncle is clever," Susan said. "But not as clever as me."

They stopped as they heard footsteps hurrying away from the cabin door. That was all they needed.

"Hurry," he said to her.

They rushed into James's bedroom and over to the window, where the climbing rope led to the second-class deck. James double-checked to make sure it was tied securely to the bed.

"That rope drops right down into the ocean, but don't you."

"Don't I what?"

"Don't fall in."

She gave him a reassuring look. "I'm an expert climber, remember?"

"I still don't like this," he said, "not one bit. Maybe the paintings aren't hidden in second class at all."

"You know they are. It's the perfect place for him to hide them. That's why you caught him wandering around the other night in second-class territory. He was checking his stolen goods." She gave him a quick kiss and began to squeeze through the window.

It was a warm night. She could see the outline of an iceberg in the water as she managed to get both arms out the window and grab the rope for support. But it was a very tight fit. She wriggled a little, but that only made it worse.

"Having trouble?" James asked from inside.

"Just a little," she called out. Her eyes followed the length of the rope as it swung in the breeze, hundreds of feet down to the ocean below. She thought about how awful it would be to be dangling from the other end, being pulled along through that frigid watcr. But right now, she had the opposite problem. "I'm stuck," she called.

"Hold on," he said. "I'm going to give you a push."

"Wait," she said, "I think I can wiggle out."

But James didn't hear her. "On the count of three," he said.

"Don't bother," she said, "I'm free."

"One . . ."

"I said don't bother."

"Two . . ."

"James!" she ordered. "Do not push me."

"Three!"

She felt like a spaceship being launched toward the moon. Shooting from the porthole with incredible force, Susan flew out in an arc. "Ahhhh!" she screamed as she saw herself swinging around, heading right at a group of portholes. She hit an open window, grabbed it for dear life, and steadied herself. "Phew, that was close!"

James stuck his head out his window ten feet away and looked around for her.

"Over here," she waved.

The look on his face was indescribable.

"I'm fine," she said, not really believing it, but feeling the need to reassure him. "I just have to swing until I'm even."

"I'll help you."

She was just preparing to let go when she was spotted by someone inside the nearest cabin.

"George! It's that wretched girl, that stowaway."

"Mrs. Winchester!" Susan exclaimed.

Mrs. Winchester looked at Susan in disdain.

Susan looked back at her in utter fear.

"George!"

"I'm coming, Marian. What is it?"

Mrs. Winchester turned and looked at her husband. "That wretched little girl is outside our window."

Her husband looked at her skeptically. "Have you been imbibing again?"

"Don't be ridiculous. It's true, I tell you. She's flying around outside our window like Peter Pan."

"Time for my exit," Susan said. "Good-bye, Mrs. W. I have to be leaving now for Never-Never Land." But in her haste to escape, Susan pushed off too hard. She flung down under James's window and back around to the cabin window on the other side. Once again she managed to grab hold of an open window.

"Thank goodness it's a warm night," she said. "Otherwise these windows would be closed and I'd be swinging for my life."

James was once again ten feet from her. His face registered sheer panic.

The sound of Mrs. Winchester's voice carried in the wind. "But she was there. I saw her."

Susan laughed. As she steadied herself on the window, she prepared to swing down more slowly this time.

James was a nervous wreck. "Are you all right?" he said in a hoarse whisper. "Can you get down to second class?"

"I think so," she said. She was just preparing to lower herself when she happened to glance into the bedroom of the cabin next door. There was James's uncle, apparently in a great hurry. Susan watched cautiously as he rummaged through his belongings, looking for something. She could see that he was perturbed, and she watched as his movements became frantic. Suddenly he found what he was looking for.

"Oh, my God," she whispered. "He's got a gun."

CHAPTER
Ten

"HE'S GOT A WHAT?" James asked.

Susan waited until Henry left his cabin. "A gun," she said, her face growing pale.

"That's it. The plan's off. Get back in here."

"I've got to hurry. I can just beat him down."

"Didn't you hear me? The plan is off. Now get back in here before you get yourself killed!"

It was too late for that. Susan waved him off and began slowly to swing under him. Without further mishap, she managed to lower herself carefully to the second-class deck. Her arms were very tired by now, but her heart began to settle down as her foot touched the railing. A moment later her other foot followed suit.

She gave James a quick salute, and then after making sure she wasn't seen, she jumped onto the deck, very relieved. And not a moment too soon. As she turned around, there was James's uncle, standing at the stern railing, staring out into the passing wake as if he hadn't a care in the world. He looked so passive that she hesitated. Something must be wrong.

A voice out of nowhere greeted her cordially. "Good evening, Ms. Melinka."

Susan whipped around and stared at the figure of Captain Gerard as he came out of the shadows of the stairwell. He seemed to be grinning—at her. "Out for an evening swing?" he asked. From the look on his face, she could tell he was not amused. "Mr. Winchester thought his wife was hallucinating. But I thought differently. What do you think?" He came up to her and smiled. She knew it was all over.

"Uh, you're not going to believe me," she said, "but I was following the art thief." She turned to look at the stern railing, but Henry was gone.

"Were you?"

"Yes. But now he's gone." She knew she sounded ridiculous, and the captain looked very impatient and increasingly angry. "You see, I had this plan."

Captain Gerard smiled without a trace of humor. "Ah, I see. You had a plan to catch the thief, but I came along and ruined it."

"Well, yes," she said uneasily, feeling more and more foolish. "I mean no. I was too late." She looked at him plaintively. "But that's not *your* fault."

He passed a weary hand across his forehead. "I'm glad to hear it. What I would like to know now is what you were doing out of your cabin. Didn't I expressly say that you were to have an escort at all times?"

At that moment James hurried up. He saw her predicament, but Susan did not want him involved. She shook her head firmly at him, but he marched right up to her and put his arm around her.

"Well, well, Mr. Bentley," the captain said. "Good of you to join us. You'll never believe who I just saw hanging around." He walked over to the railing and grabbed the dangling rope. Looking upward, he traced its path and addressed James again.

"It appears to be attached to something in your cabin, sir. Were you being robbed, or were you a partner in this endeavor?"

"He was being robbed," Susan blurted out.

"That's not true," James said. "I was helping her to climb down to second class."

"We do have elevators that work just as well as ropes," the captain said.

Susan knew that it would do no good to explain. She shut her eyes for a moment, and when she opened them the captain was summoning two very imposing seamen. "Would you both be so kind as to escort Ms. Melinka to her accommodations?" he said sternly. "And this time," he added, "throw away the key."

"This is ridiculous. She isn't guilty of anything. Can't we discuss this reasonably?" James asked. "I'm sure there is a perfectly sensible explanation."

"I'm sure there's an explanation, but I doubt that it is sensible," the captain said to James. "This young woman was in your care, sir, and you deliberately disregarded my express orders."

"And for that I duly appologize, Captain, but—"

Captain Gerard held up a hand. "No buts about it."

He gestured out at the ocean. "Look around you, sir. What do you see?"

Susan and James both looked. The rising moon cast an eerie light on the forest of icebergs, which seemed to have grown.

"Good Lord, there must be hundreds of them," Susan breathed.

"There are eight," the captain said. "But there are hundreds to come—all from the north and all because of this blasted warm weather, which we didn't expect. It's an obstacle course out there, and I don't need any trouble on board." He gestured for the sailors to take her away.

Susan faced her fate bravely. "I'll see you later, James," she whispered to him. "Come to my cabin later."

"Cabin?" the captain repeated. "Who said anything about a cabin?"

Susan stared at him, and then nodded grimly. She couldn't really blame him. "James," she said. "Help."

He took her hand and went with her as the two sailors "escorted" her down a flight of stairs. And down another. And down another, into the bowels of the ship. She could hear the familiar sound of the engines rumbling, and they matched the beating of her heart. She was truly afraid now, not just for herself, but for James as well. His uncle was desperate, and he had a gun.

The familiar cell door swung open with a noisy creak. Susan walked in and the door was pushed closed, but only halfway.

The sailors looked at each other. "It's stuck," one of them said.

"It must be rusty. I'll give you a hand."

Together the two sailors put their elbows into it and strained until it finally closed.

James looked at Susan's white face and then at the two seamen. "Will you be able to open it again?" he demanded.

They gave each other a shrug and looked at James with a laugh.

"The captain has the only key," the first one said. "If you're worried, I suggest asking him to have it fixed in the morning."

"In the morning?" Susan wailed.

"He's very busy, miss. Those icebergs are keeping all of us on our toes."

James put his arm through the bars and took her hand. "Cheer up. At least now I know you'll be safe." He pointed at the cell window. "You'd better close that before you get drenched again like last time."

"I will." She looked at him. "Be careful," she said.

"Don't worry," he answered. "I know exactly what I'm doing. Nothing can go wrong."

As if Providence had heard him, there was a sudden great crunching sound, as though the ship had suddenly run aground.

Susan froze and looked at James. He looked as petrified as she felt. Their hands squeezed until the blood left them both.

The noise inside the hull was so loud that it drowned out the sound of the engines. The force was even greater. Their hands were forced apart by a second collision, and Susan fell backward onto the floor.

Outside her window something huge seemed to glide

by. As it did, it banged and scraped hideously at the ship, depositing fragments of ice and spewing missiles of ice chips onto the floor of her prison. The noise below the hull was now deafening. Susan was paralyzed with fear.

And James was no longer outside her window.

"James," she called hysterically. "James!"

But the noise drowned out her voice. It seemed to start in the bow and make its way along to the stern until finally it left them. When she looked out her porthole, she could see part of a monstrous iceberg receding in the wake of the ship.

"James?" She waited. "James!"

Two hands managed to grab on to the windows of her cell. They were followed by his face. He checked to see that she was all right. Then he looked around outside her cell.

"What are you looking for?" she asked.

He didn't answer. Not at first. Whatever it was he was searching for, he seemed glad that he didn't find it. When at last he looked back at her, he was smiling crookedly.

"What were you looking for?" she asked again.

James took a deep breath and let it out slowly. "Holes," he said matter-of-factly. "The kind icebergs make in ships. You know. As in big, wrenching, gaping holes followed by a torrent of ocean water."

"Like the *Titanic?*" she asked in horror.

He shook his head. "Don't worry, this is a modern ship. Practically unsinkable."

Susan groaned. "That's what they said about the *Titanic!*"

"Well, nothing is unsinkable," he said. "But this one is built to last."

"They all are," she countered, and groaned again. "And the captain was telling me at dinner that they don't build them like they used to."

He smiled reassuringly. "Don't worry. We just took a tremendous bashing and we're still floating."

But Susan wasn't fooled. She looked at his face, and she knew that he was just as afraid as she was.

"James?" she asked tremulously. "Would you get me something?"

He turned the full force of his smile on her, and even now, in this awful predicament, it caused a strange little flutter within her breast. "Anything," he promised. "What is it?"

"Oh, James," she said, her heart in her voice. *"Get me out of here!"*

It started out as a small trickle.

At first Susan thought that someone had left a faucet dripping somewhere, and now it was overflowing—into her cell.

But she was wrong.

It was just a tiny, insignificant stream that no one would ever notice. But after about ten minutes, it was no longer a stream. It was more like a small tributary, growing every second. Susan had no illusions about what this meant, and her concern grew into panic.

"We're sinking," she yelled. But her voice could not carry over the hum of the engines. She tried anyway. "Help! Somebody . . . anybody . . . we're sinking!!"

Sticking her head out the porthole, she tried calling

up for help. All she got for her troubles was a soaked head as a wave crashed over her. She wiped her face and tried again.

"Anybody up there? We're sinking!"

A strong breeze was blowing her hair around wildly. She brushed it aside and gazed down at the moonlit ocean's reflection on the side of the ship. The water was only twenty-five feet below her window, and she wondered how long it would be before it was twenty feet . . . then fifteen, ten, five . . . Her heart froze at the thought of a watery grave.

Her only hope was James, and she prayed that he sensed the danger in time to save her. Blowing out a shaky breath, she pulled her head back inside and checked the floor. It was now fully covered with water.

While Susan was praying in the hull of the ship, James was hundreds of feet above her, trying desperately to get to the bridge in order to talk to the captain—and getting nowhere.

"He's a very busy man right now, sir," the purser explained as he nudged James away from the stairway that led to the bridge.

"What is happening?" James demanded.

But the purser said nothing.

Other passengers were just as eager to hear news. Panic was starting to set in as harried men in black tie and women in gowns started donning orange life preservers. They began crowding around the hapless purser, who was visibly worried, although he wouldn't admit that anything was wrong.

Mr. Winchester elbowed by James in his life preserver. "Now look here, my good man. All we want to know is whether or not there will be enough lifeboats for everyone."

A wave of agreement rumbled through the crowd.

"I'm sure everything will be fine," the purser said again, trying to calm them down. "There's no need for lifeboats. The ship is not sinking. It would take more than a scrape with an iceberg to put a hole in her."

"I don't believe you!" someone shouted boldly. "You're not telling us everything."

"And where are the lifeboats?" another person asked, confused.

"Oh, don't worry about that. We have more than enough."

Mr. Winchester snorted. "There's not a lifeboat to be seen on the upper deck. That blasted mountain of ice shaved them right off the ship!"

James was startled to hear this. He looked overhead where the lifeboats had been neatly hung along the side of the ship. All that was left of them were broken halyards and cranes and the splintered remains of now-useless lifeboats. Only two of the boats remained in the upper deck. One was hanging by a frayed rope, and it dangled dangerously back and forth above the heads of the unsuspecting passengers.

He pointed up at it just in time to warn the group that was standing under it. "Zeebo," he yelled. "Get yourself and your group away from that boat before it crashes down on you."

Zeebo looked up, and not a moment too soon. The lifeboat dangled and floated back and forth with the sway of the ship. It creaked and protested as the ropes were dragged again and again against the side of the ship, becoming more and more frayed. Then, with a snap that sounded like a firecracker, the rope split. The boat came crashing down onto the deck, and Zeebo just managed to pull a witless Oliver away from the danger.

No one was hurt, but the incident sent a flood of new panic among the passengers.

At that decisive moment, James burst past the purser and bounded up the stairs three at a time.

"Please, sir," the purser called, running after him. But he wasn't fast enough.

James stood on the top deck and gasped in horror.

The entire roof of the bridge had been shaved off. Huge blocks of ice were strewn everywhere along with jagged glass fragments and pieces of rope. Debris of all kind was scattered across the walkway. He could easily make out parts of the second-class deck below through the gaping holes in the roof. The lifeboats lower down seemed intact. He counted as many as he could, wondering if they could hold a double load of passengers. Already the second-class passengers were in their life jackets, and a few of the lifeboats were being readied over the side.

"Sir!" The purser called to him. "I must insist."

James looked inside the bridge had the captain was giving orders. Only a few small lights were operating on the control panels, and they reflected blue and red and yellow patches on the captain's face. His worried expression was enough to tell James that they were in a lot of trouble.

"Captain!" he yelled. "Captain Gerard!"

"Please, sir." The purser was now dragging at James's lapel with more than polite force.

James gave him a shove that sent him staggering backward, and banged on the door to the bridge.

"I must have the key to Susan's cell!"

The captain stopped what he was doing and looked at James.

"The key, sir," James demanded. "Susan Melinka is in danger."

The captain hesitated and then beckoned him in.

When James entered the small room, his mouth fell open. "Oh, my God!" he exclaimed.

The entire bridge was an array of broken glass, smashed valves, splintered wood, shattered equipment, and smoking fires. What had once been the steering wheel was now just a tangled mesh of gears and wires. The radio—what was left of it—lay flat on the floor, the microphone still dangling from the neck of the operator, who was bleeding from a gash above his eye.

The ship was at a complete standstill. James looked out at the surrounding ocean, and his eyes widened. The entire sea was filled with icebergs, hundreds of them. They stretched into the horizon, like ghostly visitors from another planet who had come to wreak havoc on the people of Earth. Silent, menacing, and starkly beautiful, they sat waiting for their prey.

Still, James knew that it was possible to steer around each one with effort and skill. The moon was full, there wasn't a cloud in the sky, and the ship had had the best navigation equipment available. James looked at the captain with great concern and doubt. "You'd have to have been asleep at the wheel to let this happen," he surmised.

"Or else someone was holding a gun to my head," Captain Gerard said calmly.

"Don't be ridiculous," James retorted.

The captain was unmoved. "Would you like to hear a simpler explanation?"

"Is there one?"

"I'm afraid not, nephew."

James whipped around and stared into the dark at the figure of a man with a gun in his hand. The man took a few small steps forward into the light.

"Oh, Uncle," James said, mortified. "First you resort to common burglary, and now this?"

Henry grimaced. "Please don't lecture me, James. This is hardly the time."

James stared at him, sickened by what had happened. "Were you that desperate that you had to place people's lives in danger?" He tried to move closer in an attempt to get the gun, but his uncle flinched and aimed the barrel straight at James's head.

"Now don't do anything foolish."

The captain came forward and bravely placed himself between the gun and James. "He's smashed every radio on this ship."

James could only ask one thing. He looked at his uncle sadly, and spread his hands in exasperation. *"Why?"*

"For your mother, dear boy."

"What the devil are you talking about?"

Henry explained. "I can't have my sister being haunted for the rest of her life by scandal and humiliation. Not after all she has been through in her life. It's better that she and the rest of the world think you and I went down bravely like the gentlemen we have always been."

"You're crazy! What about the other innocent people aboard this ship? Is that honorable?"

"Only you and I, the captain, and these officers know about my bungling . . ." He stopped and added one more. "Oh, and of course, your little playmate. But she won't be giving us trouble too much longer."

James felt a rising tide of dread. He would have begged and pleaded with his uncle, but he knew that would do no good.

A sudden, horrifying sound turned them all into frozen statues. It sounded like the moaning of a banshee; then it broke into a scream. They could hear the sudden crunching sound of metal. Everyone remained stock-still as something scraped right under them on the hull, hundreds of feet below them. There was a sudden but gentle pitch as the angle of the deck shifted slightly, followed by the creaking of pulleys and the banging of furniture and everything else that wasn't tied down. The passengers could be heard muttering nervously on the decks below.

The captain looked over his shoulder at a broken glass dial, and heaved a sigh.

"We're taking on water aft." He looked at the purser. "Abandon ship."

The purser looked at Henry, and then at the captain.

The captain addressed Henry with considerable dignity. "I'll go down with my ship," he said, "but I will not take innocent people with me." At those words, he reached decisively yet cautiously for the microphone.

James watched the captain's hand on the microphone

and his uncle's hand on the gun. The moment was very tense, and no one noticed as he deftly slipped his hand into the captain's large outer pocket and pulled out a set of keys.

"This is the captain speaking." He paused and looked at Henry before pronouncing the fate of everyone on board. "Abandon ship!"

It was at that precise moment that James dived out the door. The last thing he remembered was two loud shots being fired at him. He fell face down on the stairs, rolled over twice, hit his head on the metal banister, and came to a final landing on a soft cushion that he later recalled smelled of champagne. There were multicolored signal lights reflected crazily in the sky like a sudden Fourth of July, and his last thoughts were of Susan and how happy she would be when he rescued her.

CHAPTER *Eleven*

SUSAN HAD ALSO HEARD the gunfire. She looked out the porthole and saw the signal flares lighting up the sky. Then she looked down to the ocean, now only nine or ten feet below.

Please, James. I don't want to die. Not now, not when I've finally found you. She pulled her head back inside and surveyed her surroundings. Already the water on the floor was a few inches deep. It was freezing cold, and she had to sit up on the bunk to avoid getting her feet numb. She looked at the steel door to her cell and tried not to think about drowning. But the only image she could conjure up was her last bubbling breaths escaping her lifeless body as it floated down two miles to a watery grave at the bottom of the ocean.

Only hours ago she had been debating whether or not

she could handle the life of a millionaire. Now she only dreamed about living.

A sudden smashing of metal against iceberg sounded like a drum from inside the hull.

"Help!" she screamed.

As if in direct answer to her cry, a sailor peered through the cell door. "Don't worry, miss, I had one of my boys phone the captain. We'll have you out in no time. We just need the key."

"Are we going to sink?"

He didn't answer her quickly enough. "I'll go and see what's holding him up."

A long five minutes went by. Susan was losing hope. She now missed the gentle hum of the engines. That and James's voice reassuring her that everything was going to be all right. Suddenly she heard voices. "James?" she called out through the cell window. "Is that you?"

But the voices were not coming from the ship. Curiously, she turned around and stared out the porthole.

After getting a few backsplashes from waves in her face, she wiped her eyes and made out the outline of a boat.

A flare went off suddenly above it and she could now see that there were five lifeboats. All were rowing away from the ship. They were filled with passengers.

"Hey!" she waved, but they were too far away to hear her. "Hey, over here!" She tried desperately, but no one heard her.

"James!" she screamed in utter frustration. *"Please!"*

There was no answer, just the creaking of the ship as it shifted slightly to port. She was on port, and with the shift, she ran to the window again.

"Oh, my God," she gasped. Panic gripped her as she stared straight down at the ocean, now only four or five feet from the window. She could see small waves riding in sets toward her. The first one hit with enough power to send a small torrent splashing into her cell. She managed to jump back in time to keep from getting soaked. The second and third waves were not as bad, but she knew time would take care of that.

"In an hour or less," Susan said aloud. She tried not to blame James if he was too afraid to come down here. But try as she might, she couldn't help herself.

"James!" she called again in a futile effort. "I will never forgive you!" She realized hauntingly that she might not have that option. "You'll never forgive yourself!" she amended, growing hysterical. She was saying crazy things, but she had to say something, *do* something, to keep herself active. She couldn't just sit here and wait like a sheep in line for slaughter.

But James was in no position to hear her. He awoke slowly, found an empty bottle next to his head and a discarded jacket lying on the floor. The deck was deserted. He looked up to the bridge and saw the captain still standing there, confronting his uncle.

Trying to gather his wits about him, he looked at his watch. His heart stopped when he saw the time. Over twenty-five minutes had gone by. The crisis on the bridge was not as important as Susan. Nothing was as important as her. Not just because there was a life at stake, but because he knew that he didn't want to go on living if she didn't. She had come into his life like a beacon, and now he thought he would wither and die if anything happened to her.

He began to panic when he realized that the ship was now listing at an angle of at least fifteen degrees to port. "Susan's cell is on the port side," he said aloud. Rushing to the railing, he almost fell over. "Susan," he yelled down.

Two pairs of hands pulled him away from the danger as Zeebo and Oliver tried to stop him.

"We came back to find you," Zeebo said anxiously. "Are you all right? That's a nasty cut on your head."

The jangle of keys in his pocket underscored his mission. "Susan," was all he said. "She's locked in the cell in the hull."

Zeebo absorbed this information with grave horror. He shook his head solemnly. "I'm sorry, James. You've been out for quite a while. It's too dangerous to go down there now."

James almost threw him overboard in his desperation. "Get out of my way, then. I've got to try."

"It's madness!" Zeebo stood in his path, and Oliver grabbed him in an armlock.

"Let me go!" he shouted like a wild man.

"It's too late for her!" Zeebo said, holding on to James. "Look around you. There's hardly anyone left on board and there's only one more lifeboat. We're just waiting for the captain to come down off the bridge. We have to leave now. We can't risk the undertow when the ship sinks."

With a final shove, James knocked both of them to the floor. "I don't care!" He ran for the stairway like a madman in front of a stampede of elephants. Jumping four and five steps at a time, he ran down level after level. By now the ship was listing perilously. The horrible creaking continued, and as he approached the engine room, he realized he had only minutes left.

"I hope I'm not too late."

But he was.

James was only twenty feet from where the cell had been. Now there was only water. Staggering from the shock of the sight, he put the keys back in his pocket and collapsed on the stairway as water slowly rose all around him. At that moment, he didn't care if he lived or died.

But Susan did. She wanted him alive long enough so that she could throttle him.

She was dangling from a rope off the side of the ship about ten feet above where her cell window had lately been. Just half a minute before she had been squeezing out of it, pulling on the rope that swung past her porthole. She gazed up into the moonlit night, following the length of rope where it disappeared inside James's cabin.

"Thank God for small miracles," she said. "I should have known this thing would come in handy."

A wave splashed against the hull, spewing drops at her. It was enough to make her scurry even faster up the rope until at last she managed to pull herself up and over the railing.

The sight that greeted her was spooky. There wasn't a soul around. She looked out into the ocean and saw the parade of lifeboats all rowing away from the ship, dodging the hundreds of icebergs. The air was exceptionally warm, which was a blessing, and as she stood recouping her strength and breath for a moment, she wondered if James was in one of those lifeboats.

If he was, she wanted him to hear something. She wanted everyone to hear it. More pragmatically, she wanted someone to come back and get her. She looked around for some kind of megaphone to amplify her voice, but found nothing. Maybe the captain's cabin. Yes, she remembered he had a bullhorn.

Racing up the stairs two at a time, she made her way into the captain's quarters. There was the bullhorn.

She took it calmly in her hand and, feeling a crazy sense of relief, she walked slowly out and down the deck.

When she reached the railing, she lifted it to her mouth, and let everyone know what she was thinking.

"James William Bentley," she announced to the immediate population. The words boomed out and echoed magnificently off the icebergs. It was like being in an enchanted ocean forest. The moon glistened off the diamondlike floating mountains, and the sea lapped gently against the hull of the sinking ship. "James William Bentley! I know you're out there." She waited a moment before letting him have it. "You traitor! I hate you. Do you hear me?" The sound of a flare being shot from behind her made her turn suddenly.

There was an unsteady Oliver, his silhouette illuminated by the glare. He held the flare gun in one hand, and a bottle of champagne in the other.

"You're looking well, Susan." He shifted his weight from side to side, grabbed the railing for support, and raised the bottle to toast her.

"Oliver . . . have you seen James?"

Oliver pointed crookedly to the broken stairs leading

to the bridge. "Last time I saw him, he was on top of me. Used me for a landing site, he did."

"What was he doing?"

"Doing?" Oliver looked at her as if she were crazy. "Doing?" he repeated. "He was doing what had to be done."

Susan was getting nowhere with him. "Don't you understand what I'm asking?"

Oliver was not entirely lucid. She watched as he lifted the flare gun dangerously aloft. Mistaking it for the champagne bottle, he placed the barrel directly in his mouth.

She was on him in a flash. She knocked it sideways out of his mouth, just before it went off with a loud bang. The entire deck was soon phosphorescent, lit by the out-of-control rocket.

Suddenly she heard a second shot, and then a third. As the flare continued to burn, she could hear the sound of fighting above her. Then everything became quiet, except for the crackle of the flare. Looking up, she saw the captain's face emerge over the railing. He gazed down at her.

"Well, well, if it isn't Ms. Melinka."

"I'm sorry about that flare gun," she said. "Oliver slipped. Are you all right, Captain?"

"Quite," he said with a distinct sigh of relief. He held up Henry's gun. "That is, I'm all right now. Thanks to you."

"To me?" Susan said. "You're thanking me?"

The captain shook a finger at her. "Don't push your good fortune, young lady."

Henry suddenly appeared, looking down over the

railing at her. "Ah, yes, it's that troublesome young woman James was having an affair with." He gave her a condescending smile. "How are you, my dear?"

Susan saw to her astonishment that he was in handcuffs. He leaned over the railing and displayed them almost proudly for her to see.

"Where is that nephew of yours?" she asked angrily.

Henry smiled at her again and gestured with his face toward the lifeboats, which were moving farther and farther away. Captain Gerard then escorted him down the other side. The ship was listing severely to port.

"One more lifeboat left," the captain said. "Come along now, Ms. Melinka."

"I'll be with you in a minute."

"Now!" the captain barked. "Don't tempt me to leave you behind . . . because I will."

The boat shifted dangerously five degrees more and she could feel the nose diving in. Looking forward, she saw that a monstrous iceberg was drifting about a mile away, right in front of them.

Ignoring the captain, she raised the bullhorn to her mouth. "James William Bentley." She waited a second, grabbed the flare gun, and shot one up. It lit the night sky with dramatic intensity. "Which lifeboat are you on, you coward?" she called into the bullhorn. "Show your face! You hear me? Where are you?"

She put the bullhorn down and watched and waited.

The captain's voice was beyond the breaking point. "Ms. Melinka. It's now or never."

Susan followed the group to the last boat and got in with the rest of the crew and the others—Zeebo, Oliver, Henry, the purser, and Captain Gerard. She still had the bullhorn in her hand and planned to use it as soon as she spotted James.

The captain ordered the boat down, and it began to lower into the water. Susan was still seething, concentrating on what she was going to do to James when she found him. "I'll tell his mother what he did. That should get to him," she muttered.

Henry gave her a disdainful look. "You'll tell his mother nothing," he said sternly. "Our family affairs are hardly your concern."

Her temper flared. "Oh, I'm not first-class enough for you, is that it? Do me a favor. Tell James that he's a first-class coward."

Henry turned away, too haughty to argue with her. The boat hit the water, the captain pushed away, and the engine sprang into life. He steered it along the huge hull of the ship, and around the stern to portside.

As they rounded the stern, Susan saw the huge propellers sticking halfway out of the water, looking as lifeless and defeated as the ship. Her eyes followed the graceful line of the stern, moving upward until they suddenly caught sight of a very familiar object.

There was her hideout, looming high above her. The huge piece of canvas was covering something that hadn't been visible from the deck. Looking at it from the bottom, she saw that it was a huge hunk of rubber. Staring up at it with private fondness, she shook her head, remembering how well it had sheltered her. Unfortunately, she also remembered the conversation that she and James had had there, and a stab of fresh hurt overtook her.

She looked away and saw Henry's face. He was

looking up at the canvas also, just as intently as she had been.

"That raft was my hideaway for a few days," she said aloud.

Henry was watching it like a hawk, his eyes registering a grave disappointment.

"Raft?" she repeated. She hadn't even realized she had called it a raft, but from this angle, that's obviously what it was. Henry looked at her and smiled ironically.

Susan hit her head with her hand. The huge thing that she had hid in was a rubber raft. Her mind began clicking at top speed, putting it all together. A raft was a perfect getaway vehicle for someone who had to leave the ship quickly and furtively when they reached New York. It was a getaway raft—for an art thief who needed to row to the shore with millions of dollars in stolen art. One look at Henry's face staring at the raft, then his look of confession at her, told her that she was right.

"Turn this boat around," she ordered.

"What?" the captain said. "We'll do no such thing."

"But I know where the paintings are!"

Zeebo stood up in the boat and looked at her as if she had just seen God.

"Sit down, Mr. Molinari," the captain ordered.

"But my paintings!"

The lifeboat steered around to the other side of the ship, which now listed heavily, its nose pointing down. She could see that the water was now coming over the bow. In less than ten minutes it would be under the water.

"Please, Captain," Zeebo pleaded. "What harm could it do?"

They were only ten feet from the ship. Susan dipped her hand into the water to test the temperature.

"Don't even think of attempting it, Ms. Melinka," the captain warned.

"I might," Zeebo said, adding sadly, "but I can't swim."

"I can," Oliver said. "But I don't have to." He laughed a high, silly laugh. "Just ask James to do it."

Susan's heart lurched at the mention of James, and she struggled to hide her reaction.

"Just ask James to get what?" James's voice asked.

Susan's head whirled around, and she almost fell out of the boat. *"James?"*

Everyone began talking at once, and Susan looked up to see James, still elegantly attired in black tie, leaning coolly against the stair railing of the second-class deck. Only ten feet away from him, the ocean was pouring in inch by inch as the ship continued to point its way down into the sea.

His face lit up like a beacon when he saw her. "Susan! You're not dead!" he cried.

"Where have you . . . What have you . . ."

"I went down to get you," he said. "But I was too late. I thought . . ." His face crumpled for a moment, and her heart contracted.

"Oh, James," was all she could say. She remembered that she had recently informed everyone who had been on the ship that James William Bentley was a traitorous rat.

She lifted the bullhorn to her mouth, and addressed

the scattered passengers. "Now hear this," she barked to the people in the other lifeboats. "I made a mistake. James Bentley is not a coward. He's a wonderful, brave, dear man who risked his life to save me."

"Ms. Melinka," the captain hollered. "Will you please shut up?"

Susan put the bullhorn down and readied herself, just as the boat came alongside the ship next to James. In a second she sprang aboard, and James caught her.

The captain was furious. "Ms. Melinka! Get back here, now!"

But she was not to be swayed. She grabbed onto James in great excitement. "I know where the paintings are." She went into a rapid explanation that made James's jaw drop in astonishment. He looked at the captain.

"I must retrieve them, sir," he said staunchly. "For the honor of my family. And for the benefit of the world."

Susan looked at the captain, her heart in her face, and Zeebo added his pleas to hers. "Priceless art," he reminded the captain. "Irreplaceable."

"Very well," the captain said with the greatest reluctance. "But remember, that ship is going down, and if we're anywhere near her when she does, we'll all be going with her."

"Come on!" Susan called to James, and they ran.

They sprinted up to the second-class stern, the water rising every second to claim them. She could hear the captain saying something about what he was going to do to her when he got hold of her again, but it was lost in the tension of the moment.

"We made it," she said as they both walked up the angled deck one step at a time to the railing. A moment later they were over the side climbing down until they landed carefully on the rubber surface. The captain had brought his boat back around and was now directly under them. Only one problem remained.

"I forgot," James said with a groan as he lifted the chain. "It's locked."

The captain called up. "You have my keys!"

It was true. James had taken the ring of keys from the captain when he had been on his way to rescue Susan. He reached into his pocket and retrieved them, but their excitement died when they saw them. There were over fifty of them.

"Hurry," Susan said frantically.

James began trying each one. Precious seconds ticked by as he inserted one at a time, tried to turn the lock, and failed.

While he was doing this, Susan began untying the raft from the hull of the ship. The captain's lifeboat was getting closer as the ship sank faster and faster. Huge bubbles began popping up from underneath.

"You'll never make it," the captain yelled. "I order you to leave that ship immediately. I cannot stay here much longer. The undertow will take us all down."

"We're not leaving until we get those paintings," Susan yelled back at him.

Zeebo was standing up in the boat, watching them tensely.

"Hurry up," Oliver muttered. "We have to get out of here."

"Shut up, Oliver."

"I must leave now," the captain warned them.

Suddenly there was the unmistakable sound of a lock clinking open.

"Got it!" James announced.

Then they felt the entire raft begin to slide down the side of the stern.

"Oh, no," Susan said as she watched the chain run through James's hand.

The last link clunked against the ship, and there was nothing left between them and the ocean.

"Hold on," James cried out, and he lunged for her hand just as the raft made the final plunge into the icy water.

"I've got you!" he called, pulling her onto the raft. Her feet and legs felt the sting of the icy chill, but James quickly pulled the tarp over them, and they were safe.

Susan looked up and froze. There were the huge propellers of the ship looming menacingly above them. Any second the ship would take its final dive, and the propellers would come down on them.

Someone threw a rope from the captain's boat, and Susan grabbed it in time. The captain put his motor into gear and a moment later they were being pulled to safety, away from the ship.

They all stared at the awesome sight of the gigantic ship as she slowly, inevitably, disappeared foot by foot like a great white coffin into the sea.

No one spoke for several minutes. Then the captain said, "Thank God we're all safe."

"You got the paintings," Zeebo said, closing his eyes in gratitude.

"Did we?" Susan asked, reorienting herself as she shivered in the ocean air.

"Let's take a look," James said, giving her shoulders a squeeze.

He reached into the raft, fumbled around for a breathless moment, and came up with the tubes containing the stolen paintings. He held them aloft for Zeebo to see.

Zeebo said nothing, his face starting to fold in on itself. Susan saw that there were tears in his eyes. "Thank you," was all he could manage. "Thank you a million times."

Susan fell back against James, suddenly exhausted. "It's over," she breathed, beginning to tremble. "Oh, James, I thought you weren't going to come. I thought you didn't care."

His arms tightened around her protectively. "Are you serious? I got knocked out for a while, and when I finally made it down there, the cell was filled with water." He stopped for a moment, his face drawn. His voice was shaky when he continued. "I thought . . . I thought you were . . ." He couldn't finish. "I didn't want to go on living then, myself. I sat on the steps for a long time before I managed to stumble out of there. The ship could have sunk right then, and I wouldn't have cared."

"Oh, James," she whispered, her voice breaking. "I wouldn't have wanted you to do that."

"I wasn't thinking clearly. All I knew was that I had lost you, and I didn't want to go on without you."

Her heart leaped with sudden happiness. "Do you mean that, James?"

He looked down into her eyes and tenderly pushed a

tendril of golden hair away from her face. "I love you, Susan. I don't know how it happened, but it did. I don't want you to leave me, ever."

"We're so different," she whispered, but she was smiling, her hands trembling as they reached for his.

"Not that different. We're both rascals, aren't we?"

She nodded, her eyes misting. "I was worried that I would lose all the independence I had gained."

He chided her gently, kissing her forehead. "I have no intention of standing in your way, ever. It's what I love best about you. You're a free spirit."

"Not that free," she said, shaking her head. "I don't want to leave you, either." She looked up and faced him, her heart in her eyes. "I love you, too, James, God help me. I don't know how I'm going to sit through those dreadful dinner parties, but I'll learn, I swear."

James laughed, his face merry once again. "Don't worry about that. I can't stand them either. I was thinking of leaving my father's business anyway. It's never been mine, always his, and I've always been caught in the middle between his family and my mother's. I'm tired of that. I want to start my own business somewhere else—anywhere. The West Coast, maybe. We can live anywhere you want, do whatever we like."

"Do you mean that?" she asked with a sly little grin.

"Of course. Why?"

"Well, I was thinking . . ." The mischievous glint he loved so well lit up her eyes.

"Oh, no. What is it? Out with it."

"Promise you won't laugh?"

"I promise."

"Well . . . I was thinking . . . I'd like to take flying lessons. I want to become a pilot."

James burst out laughing.

"James!" she cried, stung.

"I can't help it." He chuckled. "I'm not laughing at you. It's just that it's so perfect for you. I can't think of anything that would suit you more."

She threw her arms around his neck and kissed him, but the captain's voice interrupted them.

"Get over here, you two. *Now.* I've had just about enough from both of you."

"Aye, aye, sir," Susan called back earnestly. "But I think we need something for a toast. James and I have something to celebrate." As everyone watched, she reached into the raft and rummaged around until she came up with the captain's bottle of sherry. "For you, sir," she offered.

Captain Gerard groaned loudly, and everyone laughed.

"Promise me you'll always stay like this," James said to her.

She looked up at him, her eyes shining. "Always," she promised.

COMING NEXT MONTH

WINDOW ON TODAY #454
by Joan Hohl

Despite rumors that artist Jared Cradowg is a womanizer, Karla Janowitz accepts his invitation to an art-inspired tour of Arizona. They soon discover that their passion for beauty is far surpassed by their passion for each other...

STORM AND FIRE #455
by Kelly Adams

Emma Kendrick has to reconcile the brute her sister has portrayed, with the handsome, sensitive man she meets on her nephew's behalf. But even though Joel Rivers encourages Emma's company, he fears the very love she has to give.

BE SURE TO READ...

WINDOW ON YESTERDAY #450
by Joan Hohl

When Alycia Matlock awakens after her accident, somehow it's the year 1777, and her beloved Sean is a lifetime away. Then she meets Patrick Halloran—a virtual double of Sean—and Alycia finds herself torn between two men...centuries apart!

NEVER SAY NEVER #451
by Courtney Ryan

Holly McKenna would rather deny the passion she and best friend Thomas Crockett feel for each other, than risk ruining their long-standing and treasured relationship. Thomas, however, would rather teach Holly never to say never...

Order on opposite page

	ISBN	Title	Price
___	0-425-10225-4	**TWO'S COMPANY #412** Sherryl Woods	$2.25
___	0-425-10226-2	**WINTER FLAME #413** Kelly Adams	$2.25
___	0-425-10227-0	**A SWEET TALKIN' MAN #414** Jackie Leigh	$2.25
___	0-425-10228-9	**TOUCH OF MIDNIGHT #415** Kerry Price	$2.25
___	0-425-10229-7	**HART'S DESIRE #416** Linda Raye	$2.25
___	0-425-10230-0	**A FAMILY AFFAIR #417** Cindy Victor	$2.25
___	0-425-10513-X	**CUPID'S CAMPAIGN #418** Kate Gilbert	$2.50
___	0-425-10514-8	**GAMBLER'S LADY #419** Cait Logan	$2.50
___	0-425-10515-6	**ACCENT ON DESIRE #420** Christa Merlin	$2.50
___	0-425-10516-4	**YOUNG AT HEART #421** Jackie Leigh	$2.50
___	0-425-10517-2	**STRANGER FROM THE PAST #422** Jan Mathews	$2.50
___	0-425-10518-0	**HEAVEN SENT #423** Jamisan Whitney	$2.50
___	0-425-10530-X	**ALL THAT JAZZ #424** Carole Buck	$2.50
___	0-425-10531-8	**IT STARTED WITH A KISS #425** Kit Windham	$2.50
___	0-425-10558-X	**ONE FROM THE HEART #426** Cinda Richards	$2.50
___	0-425-10559-8	**NIGHTS IN SHINING SPLENDOR #427** Christina Dair	$2.50
___	0-425-10560-1	**ANGEL ON MY SHOULDER #428** Jackie Leigh	$2.50
___	0-425-10561-X	**RULES OF THE HEART #429** Samantha Quinn	$2.50
___	0-425-10604-7	**PRINCE CHARMING REPLIES #430** Sherryl Woods	$2.50
___	0-425-10605-5	**DESIRE'S DESTINY #431** Jamisan Whitney	$2.50
___	0-425-10680-2	**A LADY'S CHOICE #432** Cait Logan	$2.50
___	0-425-10681-0	**CLOSE SCRUTINY #433** Pat Dalton	$2.50
___	0-425-10682-9	**SURRENDER THE DAWN #434** Jan Mathews	$2.50
___	0-425-10683-7	**A WARM DECEMBER #435** Jacqueline Topaz	$2.50
___	0-425-10708-6	**RAINBOW'S END #436** Carole Buck	$2.50
___	0-425-10709-4	**TEMPTRESS #437** Linda Raye	$2.50
___	0-425-10743-4	**CODY'S GYPSY #438** Courtney Ryan	$2.50
___	0-425-10744-2	**THE LADY EVE #439** Dana Daniels	$2.50
___	0-425-10836-8	**RELEASED INTO DAWN #440** Kelly Adams	$2.50
___	0-425-10837-6	**STAR LIGHT, STAR BRIGHT #441** Frances West	$2.50
___	0-425-10873-2	**A LADY'S DESIRE #442** Cait Logan	$2.50
___	0-425-10874-0	**ROMANCING CHARLEY #443** Hilary Cole	$2.50
___	0-425-10914-3	**STRANGER THAN FICTION #444** Diana Morgan	$2.50
___	0-425-10915-1	**FRIENDLY PERSUASION #445** Laine Allen	$2.50
___	0-425-10945-3	**KNAVE OF HEARTS #446** Jasmine Craig	$2.50
___	0-425-10946-1	**TWO FOR THE ROAD #447** Kit Windham	$2.50
___	0-425-10986-0	**THE REAL THING #448** Carole Buck	$2.50
___	0-425-10987-9	**SOME KIND OF WONDERFUL #449** Adrienne Edwards	$2.50

Please send the titles I've checked above. Mail orders to:

BERKLEY PUBLISHING GROUP
390 Murray Hill Pkwy., Dept. B
East Rutherford, NJ 07073

NAME ______________________

ADDRESS ______________________

CITY ______________________

STATE ______________ **ZIP** ______________

Please allow 6 weeks for delivery.
Prices are subject to change without notice.

POSTAGE & HANDLING:
$1.00 for one book, $.25 for each additional. Do not exceed $3.50.

BOOK TOTAL	$______
SHIPPING & HANDLING	$______
APPLICABLE SALES TAX (CA, NJ, NY, PA)	$______
TOTAL AMOUNT DUE	$______

PAYABLE IN US FUNDS.
(No cash orders accepted.)

"It is reassuring to know we will pass to the other side...where we will be reunited with loved ones."
—*New York Times Book Review*

WE DON'T DIE

George Anderson's Conversations With The Other Side

THE ASTONISHING NATIONWIDE BESTSELLER!

WE DON'T DIE will change forever the way you look at life, death, and the transcendent power of love. The warmth and wisdom of George Anderson's proven gift to communicate with the spirits on "the other side," offers us all a glimpse of eternity—and the heartfelt, universal vision to know that "No one you are close to ever dies..."

A BERKLEY PAPERBACK  *ON SALE IN MARCH*